"I hope you didn't mind my waking you, Tracy. But I just had to talk to you."

"No problem, Leslie. I wanted to hear all about your date. I'm really happy for you. Now I'm looking forward to tomorrow night's installment."

"That makes two of us," Leslie answered. She lay on her bed in a trance, imagining her next date with Jeff. She pictured herself in Jeff's arms. She could almost feel his tender kisses.

Heaven, she thought. *What a perfect way to spend an evening. Why on earth did I say I didn't want to go for a drive tonight? We could have kissed all night instead of just once at the door.* She sighed. *Oh well, I had a fantastic evening anyway. Besides, there's always tomorrow.* The thought gave her a warm feeling inside. *Just don't get too carried away,* she warned herself sternly.

ENDLESS *Summer*

TOO HOT TO HANDLE
Linda Davidson

IVY BOOKS • NEW YORK

This one's for the Zeiger bunch:
Ron, Ted, Mimi, Helane, Robert, Sima,
Nina, Ari, Kalman, Reva, and Judy.
I love you all.

Ivy Books
Published by Ballantine Books
Copyright © 1988 by Butterfield Press, Inc.

Produced by Butterfield Press, Inc.
133 Fifth Avenue
New York, New York 10003

Library of Congress Catalog Card Number: 87-92139

ISBN 0-8041-0242-2

Manufactured in the United States of America

First Edition: August 1988

Chapter 1

"I'm sorry, Russ, I need the car to get to work," Leslie Stevens explained to her older brother.

Russell was in the midst of fixing himself some breakfast. He shook up a pitcher of frozen orange juice, then poured himself a glass. "I distinctly remember Dad saying the car belonged to both of us. You've had it every day since it came out of the repair shop. C'mon, Les, be fair." Russ turned on a smile full force. "When do I get my turn?"

Leslie smiled back at him and said, "Need I remind you, my dear brother, that Dad also said he was buying the car so I could get to my summer lifeguard job?"

If she had to, Leslie could also remind him that on the very same day their parents left for their trip to Europe, he had cracked up their brand-new, red Suzuki jeep. For the four weeks that the car was in the body shop, Leslie had driven into Marina Bay with Jeff, the head lifeguard and her boss. Of course she couldn't really complain about spending extra time with Jeff in his Cadillac convertible.

The other complication arising from Russ's accident had taken a little more adjustment. To pay for the car repairs, Russ had cooked up some hare-brained scheme to rent out rooms in their beach house while their parents were gone. So now every bedroom had a boarder in it, including hers. *And what a crazy crew they are,* she thought. Angelo DeFurie had arrived first. He went by the name Fury and was a wicked surfer. Pamela Easton had arrived next, but she'd hardly said a word to the rest of them since she'd installed herself in the master suite. Then came Jed Mason, Russ's talkative roommate from Berkeley. And last but not least there was Tracy Berberian, an aspiring Country Western singer who was sharing a room with Leslie. While Leslie realized that the arrangement had worked out well so far, she wasn't about to admit that to Russ. In fact, if he tried to get tough about the car, she could easily make him feel very guilty. It was kind of fun to have the upper hand, Leslie thought.

"Well, when do you think I can have the car?" Russ asked, still sweet as can be.

"I don't know."

"Take a guess."

"Look, Russ, as soon as I find out when I have a day off and don't need the car, I promise you, you'll be the first to know."

"When will that be?" Russ asked. He sounded as if he was losing his patience.

"I said I don't know." Leslie was losing hers, too. "At least the car's running. Look, can't we talk about this tonight? I've got to finish getting ready or I'll be late. Now I don't even have time to eat."

"Okay, okay, to be continued." Russ let the subject drop and went back to making his breakfast.

Leslie raced upstairs, tiptoed into her bedroom so as not to awaken Tracy, and snatched her lifeguard sweatshirt from off the back of a chair. Quickly, she pulled it on over her pink one-piece bathing suit and matching running shorts. Then she ran back downstairs and grabbed her red canvas beach bag from the coffee table in the living room.

"You shouldn't run out of the house without breakfast. Here, drink this," her brother said, walking out from the kitchen with a glass of juice in one hand and a plate of toast in the other.

"Russ, I don't have time."

"Yes you do. Now drink." Russ handed her the glass.

Leslie bolted the O. J. down.

"And I made you some toast. Here's a napkin so you can eat it on your way to work."

Leslie knew all too well what Russ was up to. What was that saying she'd heard? You can catch more bees with honey than vinegar. Something like that. Russ was definitely using the "catch the car with honey" approach on her this morning. She handed him her empty glass, folded the toast inside the napkin, and shoved it into her beachbag.

"Thanks. Gotta go," she said and headed for the front door.

Russ wasn't the only one who was doing his best to prevent her from getting to work on time. Fury, whom Jeff had recently hired as a relief lifeguard on Marina Bay Beach, was, as usual, also hanging her up.

"Fury, I'm leaving," Leslie shouted as she passed his door on her way out of the house. "If you want a ride, you'd better move it."

What takes him so long? she wondered as she fastened her seat belt. She started the engine and backed the jeep out of the carport. *If Fury doesn't get out here in a hurry, I'll have to leave without him.* Slowly she counted to ten, then just when she was about to drive off, Fury finally made an appearance.

As he slid into the seat next to her, Leslie noticed that his purple high-tops were still untied. A T-shirt, a pair of wrap-around sunglasses, and ragged cut-offs made up the rest of his unkempt outfit, along with the earrings that he was still putting in his ears.

"Aren't you afraid of losing an earring in the water?" she asked him as she drove down Sandpiper.

"So, I lose an earring. Big deal. I'd feel naked if I didn't wear them," he replied. "It's kind of like being bald, you know? I mean, you wouldn't go out of the house without your hair, would you?"

Leslie couldn't argue with that, although it was a strange comparison. Her long blond hair was her best feature, and she loved how the wind blew it every which way when she picked up speed on Surfrider Drive. In her red Suzuki, with her windswept hair and pink shades on, she knew she looked hot.

If she looked so good, then why, she now

asked herself, was she having so much trouble getting something romantic going this summer? Maybe she should have let Russ have the car after all. Then she could have gone to work with Jeff. She missed riding into town with him, but Jeff, she was sure, didn't miss her. The gorgeous hunk could have any girl on the beach he wanted. She was equally certain that she wasn't on his list, and that thought really depressed her. He was always very nice to her, but their relationship seemed to stop there. Even at the party they'd had at the beach house the week before, he'd been more interested in dancing with the other girls than with her.

Slowing down as she passed T-Shirts For Two, the T-shirt and poster store on Surfrider Drive where her roommate worked, Leslie decided to have lunch with her this afternoon.

"Are you planning to see Tracy?" Leslie asked Fury. Tracy and Fury had become a very tight couple soon after they'd met. Everyone around Leslie these days seemed to be in pairs.

"She won't be in until about ten-thirty. I'll probably stop by on my break. Why?"

"Can you ask her to meet me for lunch at one o'clock in front of Tortilla Flats? If you're not planning to have lunch with her, that is.

I'm in the mood for a hot tamale and I know how she loves Mexican food. Tell her I'll treat."

"No problem, Leslie. I'm scheduled to relieve you today around one," Fury told her.

"Great!" Leslie said.

That settled it. She'd shelve her boy problem until lunch when she could discuss it with Tracy, who was an expert on the subject of love; every Western song she knew had the word in it. She sang about pining for love, dying for love, unrequited love. Leslie wasn't sure what category she fit into, but Tracy would know, all right.

Besides, it was too nice a day to let the lack of a little love in her life get her down, not when she had everything else: the best car and job in town and, with her parents away in Europe, the whole summer to be on her own. She was feeling better already as she spotted a parking space not too far from her lifeguard tower, number four, and pulled in. The day was looking up.

"Thanks for the lift, Leslie. Don't wait for me after work. Tracy and I will probably go out later and I can get a ride home with her," Fury said as he headed over to lifeguard tower number three further down the beach.

"Don't forget to tell Tracy I'll see her at lunch," Leslie reminded him.

She grabbed her beach bag from the back-seat and headed over to the tower. Bag in tow, she climbed up to her lifeguard position on the elevated platform. Out of her bag she took her day's supplies: whistle on a sturdy cord, sun visor, zinc for her nose, suntan lotion for the rest of her body. She took off her sweat-shirt and put on the whistle and visor. Next, she painted her nose with hot pink zinc and rubbed her arms and legs with an ample amount of suntan lotion. Finally, she reached into her bag again, took out a piece of toast, and started nibbling on it.

Yuk, cold dry toast. Still, I guess it's better than nothing, Leslie thought as she checked the water to get a read on the conditions. The waves were moderate, no problem, she noted, at least not yet. And the few early morning swimmers all looked pretty strong. No one appeared tired or was looking in to shore. But it was still early. She could tell by the absence of smog and the cloudless blue sky above that today was shaping up to be one of those perfect Southern California days where the beach was the only place to be. And that's exactly where she would be from nine to five, along with at least half of Marina Bay. She'd have to stay alert. It was going to be a busy day at Marina Bay Beach. *Good*, Leslie said to herself, *no time for brooding about my nonexistent love life.*

Chapter 2

"Take this basket of chips away from me, Tracy. And the salsa. It's a good thing Russ made me some toast this morning, otherwise I'd eat the basket, too. Boy, I'm hungry. Where is our lunch?" Leslie wondered out loud.

Fury had relieved Leslie at her lifeguard station as planned, and now she and Tracy were having lunch at Tortilla Flats, the Mexican restaurant on Surfrider Drive, just up the street from T-Shirts For Two. They were seated at a booth by a beige stucco wall with Corona and Dos Equis beer signs on it and filling up on tortilla chips while waiting for their order to arrive.

"Do you mean you survived all morning with only a piece of toast?" Tracy remarked in mock surprise. "I can't believe it. Les, you're ruining your reputation as the girl with the biggest appetite in Marina Bay."

Leslie grinned. "Don't worry. Just wait until I sink my teeth into those hot tamales."

Tracy looked at Leslie curiously. "So, what's the occasion for this lunch anyway? Don't tell me—you've just rescued a record producer from drowning and as a reward he's offered to give your roommate a recording contract, right?"

Leslie shook her head. "No, sorry." Now that she had to tell it to Tracy, her problem seemed silly. "I just thought it would be fun to have lunch together."

"There must be more to it if you're treating. I've got the feeling you've got something on your mind," Tracy said.

"Pass me back the chips. I'm starving."

Tracy moved the basket far out of Leslie's reach. "Not until you 'fess up."

"Okay, okay. Let me have a chip." Leslie waited until Tracy had slid the basket to her end of the table before answering. "Well, it isn't all that important. Only that I thought, since you're such an expert on the subject, you could give me some advice."

"I'd love to, Les, if I only knew on what," Tracy replied. "Western shirts? Motorcycle parts? Guitar strings? Heart strings?"

"You've got it," Leslie interrupted.

"Heart strings, huh? C'mon, Leslie, you'll have to tell me more than that."

After one last chip, Leslie was about to explain her problem when their waitress arrived with their lunch.

"Hot tamales and a side order of refried beans for you. Careful, the plate's hot," the waitress warned, putting it in front of Leslie. "And enchilada verde and beans for you." She set another hot plate of food before Tracy.

"Okay. Here's my problem," Leslie said, deciding to level with Tracy while waiting for her hot tamales to cool. "Well, you'd think I was having a terrific summer, right? I've got a great job, a great car, no parents around. What's there to complain about, right? Wrong! I've got everything but . . ."

"A little romance in your life," Tracy broke in.

Leslie was glad now that she had decided to open up to Tracy. If anyone would understand, it was Tracy. "Okay, now that you know my problem, can you help me?" Leslie asked.

Tracy swallowed a forkful of beans. "Well, I'll be honest with you, Leslie. Someone as pretty as you should be attracting boys like flies unless you're wearing a paper bag on your head. So, you must be doing something wrong," she told Leslie candidly.

"Maybe I *should* wear a paper bag on my head. I'd probably have better luck," Leslie joked. "The thing is that I don't know what I'm doing wrong."

"I do. It's simple. You're giving off negative vibes. Getting a guy is just like, say in your case, getting straight A's or a job as the first female lifeguard on the beach. You have to put your mind to it. And your body, too," Tracy explained. "If you were putting out the right message, your body language would be saying, 'Here I am, guys.' Instead, you're saying, 'Stay away. I'm not interested.'"

Leslie nodded. What Tracy said certainly made some sense. She sounded more like Dr. Ruth than her summer roommate from Fresno. "So how do I change my body language?" she asked.

"You have to be subtle. You don't want to go too far. Just be friendly and smile a lot. Act like you want to talk, not like you're afraid," Tracy said.

"Right, I think I get it. Like this, right?"

Leslie leaned forward in her seat, her eyes alert and her lips curved into a small smile.

Tracy grinned. "See? Nothing to it. Glad I could be of help." She bit into her enchilada. "Now I've got to get to work on my lunch. I need to get back to the store soon."

Leslie glanced at her waterproof Swatch. She couldn't believe it was already a quarter of two. She had exactly fifteen minutes in which to get her lunch down.

It was five past two when she returned to her post and told Fury that he could leave. By now the beach was wall to wall with sleek, tanned bodies. Even with her new body language, how could she compete with all the girls in their high-cut monokinis and skimpy bikinis?

The afternoon waves were spilling on top of each other, and hordes of hot-shot surfers were racing across them. Leslie would have to be on guard for wipeouts and fly-away surfboards. She preferred to be on the lookout for her summer romance, but she took her job seriously. *Business before pleasure*, Leslie told herself.

But after only an hour she was getting restless and bored. She almost wished she spotted someone thrashing in the water just so she could get up from her chair and move around. What harm was there, she decided, in breaking up the monotony and experimenting with some body talk? She could still keep a careful watch.

She crossed her legs seductively, changing her message the way Tracy had advised. But the only living thing that came anywhere close to her in the next ten minutes was a sea gull. *And he's only interested in the crumbs from this morning's toast,* she realized with a dejected sigh. *If only Jeff would come by on his patrol, perhaps it would work on him.* A few minutes later, however, her bottom leg was asleep and she couldn't stand it anymore. She stood up and shook it out. So much for that signal.

She sat down in her lifeguard's chair again, put her hands on her hips, and struck a pose that she was sure said, "Here I am, guys." A nicely tanned guy in a blue Speedo walked right past her without a second glance.

Determined not to be discouraged, Leslie kept up her pose. Two long-legged girls looked up at her as they strolled by in their sexy, one-piece bathing suits. She recognized one girl from her English class. The other girl had been very popular around school, although she seemed like a real snob to Leslie.

"What's with her?" Leslie overheard the one who had been in her English class say to the other girl.

"Real stuck on herself. Worse than ever since she got the job as a lifeguard," the other replied.

"She was like that in English class, too. Just because she got straight A's she acted as if she was better than everyone else," the first girl agreed.

When Leslie caught their gaze, the two girls snapped their heads sharply in the direction they were heading and strutted past her. She got the impression that they had wanted her to hear their conversation. The guys on the beach obviously hadn't gotten Leslie's message, but Leslie had heard the girls' message loud and clear.

Jealousy, pure and simple, Leslie fumed to herself. But they had no right to be. She had trained hard to qualify for her lifeguard's position. For six years straight, while they were probably still in bed, she had already been in the pool swimming lap after lap before school even started. And like studying all night and getting an A on the test the next day, her hard work had paid off. She had come in third in the lifeguard try-outs last spring and had been chosen to be the first female life-guard on Marina Bay Beach. No, they weren't going to take away what she had rightfully earned with their petty attitude problem. Let them talk. What did she care?

But I do care, Leslie thought. "Maybe it's not my body language but my body odor," she muttered under her breath to make herself laugh. Because if she didn't laugh, she might cry. *Why is it that at every other stretch of beach, people gather around the lifeguard stand? But when I'm on duty, I have only myself to talk to?*

She pulled herself together, more deter-mined than ever to forget those dumb girls and give Tracy's suggestion another try. May-be, she thought, her mirrored sunglasses made her appear standoffish. She took them off and dropped them into her beach bag. She reprogrammed her misty blue eyes and frown-ing face back into "friendly" just in time. Jeff was heading toward her.

"How's it going this afternoon?" he shouted up to her.

"Oh, just fine. There's been surprisingly little trouble for such a crowded day. How's it going for you?" she asked in her friendliest voice. Jeff was so everything—so muscular, so tan, so athletic, so all-around buff that usually she was tongue-tied around him, but today she was making an extra effort to be bright and personable.

"So far, so good," he said with a smile. "Want to stretch your legs and patrol for a while? I'll take your tower."

"Sure. Sounds great," Leslie replied. A walk on the beach was just what she needed. By midafternoon the inactivity of sitting in a chair all day took its toll on her. But Jeff, sensitive to the needs of his staff, usually sent Fury over to give her a thirty-minute patrol break at this time of day. Today, more than ever, she welcomed it. *But why had Jeff come himself?* she wondered as she yanked her sweatshirt out of her beach bag, tied it around her waist, then joined her boss on the sand.

"Shall I come back in half an hour?" she asked.

"Take an hour. You look like you need it," he said, handing her his walkie-talkie.

"I do. Thanks, Jeff. See you at four-thirty," she replied, and headed over to where the sand was wet and easier to walk on.

When she reached the hardpacked sand, Jeff called to her, "I miss you already."

The remark caught her off guard. It seemed so out of place in their very businesslike relationship. *Do something friendly*, Leslie urged herself. *Don't pass up this opportunity to let him know you're interested*. She turned around, prepared to give Jeff a smile and a friendly wave, but he was already in her chair looking for trouble in the water and not in her direction at all.

As she patrolled the beach on the lookout for litterers, beer drinkers, beach bums, and beach bullies, she was more distracted and puzzled than ever. *Why hadn't Jeff sent Fury over to her station?* she asked herself again. Question after question ran non-stop through her head like a sixty-minute tape through a tape deck. Had Tracy's advice worked? Had he noticed her revised body language? Or was Jeff just being friendly? And what had he meant by his remark?

Probably nothing, Leslie told herself, but still she couldn't wait to get back to her post to test Jeff's reaction to the new, more approachable Leslie. Now she wished he hadn't given her the extra half hour, and when she reached Fury, who was now at tower number two, she was thankful it was time to turn around.

"Hi, Leslie," he called down to her. "How'd your lunch go with Tracy?"

"Oh, fine. Just great," Leslie replied quickly.

"That's good." Fury paused. "Hey, Les, you

haven't seen any sign of a drifter in your area, have you? He was down here earlier on, but I told him to get lost. If he causes any trouble—"

"No, I haven't seen him," Leslie interrupted. She didn't have the patience to stand there and chat. "I've got to get back. Can you tell Tracy I need to talk to her when she gets home? She can wake me if I'm asleep."

"You two sure have a lot to talk about lately. I'll give her the message," Fury assured her.

Leslie jogged back to the tower to save time. As she approached her station she saw Jeff coming down to meet her. Was he as eager to see her as she was to see him, she wondered? She put on her friendly smile and took a deep breath.

"Hi, Jeff. It's amazing. Everyone on the beach is so well-behaved today. Maybe we'll have to set a bad example," she joked in a bright tone.

"Good, you're back early," Jeff said brusquely, as if he hadn't heard one word she'd said. "I've got to make tracks over to tower number one. Can I have the walkie-talkie?" he asked, all businesslike again.

Leslie stared at him. Now she was more bewildered than before. First Jeff had given her extra time. Now he was in a big hurry to get over to tower number one at the other end of the beach. Why had he bothered to come over here in the first place? Leslie asked herself once more.

"I've got to go. The walkie-talkie?" Jeff said again.

"Oh, here, sorry." She realized she could ask herself a thousand times over what was going through Jeff's mind and she still wouldn't come up with an answer. *Guys sure are a mystery*, she decided.

Chapter 3

Leslie heard the front door slam and sleepily reached for her Swatch on the white night table that separated her bed from Tracy's. She rubbed her eyes and focused on the blurry numbers. They glowed 1:30 A.M. It was later than she'd thought. No wonder she had fallen asleep waiting up for her roommate. She listened for Tracy's footsteps on the stairs, but instead she heard Fury and Tracy enter the den downstairs. Leslie closed her eyes again. She knew it would be a while now before Tracy came upstairs.

Tracy's so lucky to have Fury, she thought

sleepily. *He may not look like much, but he's such a nice guy. They make a terrific couple.* Leslie yawned. *I bet Jeff and I would make a terrific couple, too. . . .*

She saw herself on the beach with Jeff. The sun was setting and the beach was deserted. She could see every detail of Jeff's face—his broad, tanned forehead, blue-gray eyes, and moist, inviting lips. When he wrapped his strong arms around her and drew her close to him, she knew he was going to kiss her at last. His kiss was soft, but passionate. They kissed until they ran out of breath. Now she felt his hand rest on her shoulder and heard him whisper softly in her ear, "I'm home, Les."

"Jeff?"

"Oh, you've got it bad, Leslie. No, it's me, Tracy."

"Oh, Tracy, it's you," Leslie said, forcing her eyes open again.

"Sorry to disappoint you. If you're expecting Jeff, I'll go back downstairs."

"Jeff? Why would I be expecting him?"

"Because you just said his name."

"I did? I must have been dreaming."

"Go back to sleep. We can talk in the morning. Sorry to wake you, but Fury said you wanted me to."

"No. No. That's all right. I did. As long as

Jeff's obviously on my mind, we might as well talk now. Unless you're too tired."

"We'd better talk. I'm too curious to go to sleep." Tracy turned on the night lamp above her bed. "So what's this about Jeff? You didn't tell me that part at lunch, but I could have guessed," she said as she pulled off her cowboy boots and settled herself comfortably on her bed.

Leslie propped up her pillow and sat up. "Well, this afternoon I tried sending some messages with my body, the way you said I should, but I'm not sure the technique worked."

"What do you mean you're not sure? Either it worked or it didn't."

"That's why I needed to talk to you. First it worked, then I think it backfired."

"Leslie, I'm confused."

"So am I." Leslie explained how Jeff had reacted to her when he first came over to relieve her, and how he acted later, when she came back from patrol. "So what do you make of his behavior, Tracy?"

"Hmm, hard to tell. Seems to me, he's giving you mixed messages."

"Oh, that's terrific! I'm glad I stayed up half the night waiting to hear you tell me what I had already figured out for myself."

"Okay, you want my advice?"

"I'm waiting."

"Go back to sleep. Things might work out better in your dreams than in real life."

"You're probably right. Jeff was just being cute. I guess I read too much into his remark. Is that what you think?" Leslie asked, hoping that Tracy would contradict her.

"I don't know. It's late. All of a sudden I feel really tired. Maybe we should talk in the morning," Tracy said. She sounded as if her thoughts were far away.

"You and Fury have something really nice going," Leslie remarked. Tracy's mind was obviously still on her own boyfriend.

"We sure do," Tracy said, the dreamy quality still in her voice.

"It must be nice to be able to share so many special times with a special guy," Leslie said wistfully.

"Sounds to me like you're doing a pretty good job making them up. Now go to sleep and get back to Jeff," Tracy said in her usual down-to-earth voice. "I'd better get ready for bed."

Tracy got up and pulled off her Marina Bay Beach Club T-shirt, similar to the one Fury had been wearing at work. Then she wiggled out of her tight black jeans, snatched her nightie from under her pillow, and slipped it over her head. "I'm going to wash up, then I'll turn the light out," she said before disappearing into the hallway.

Leslie scooted down under her covers and turned on her side. She closed her eyes and tried once more to follow Tracy's advice. But try as she might, she couldn't conjure up the image of her and Jeff on the beach. This time she didn't need to ask anyone what her problem was. She knew all too well. Only in her dreams was she satisfied with fantasy; when she was awake, she wanted the real thing.

Chapter 4

"Did you find out when your next day off is?"
Russ asked Leslie through the bathroom door.

"No. I told you I'd tell you as soon as I
knew."

"Do you think you could ask Jeff today? I'd
really like to know when I can use the car."

"Russ, go away. I'm trying to get ready for
work."

After being up most of the night thinking
about Jeff's weird behavior yesterday, she was
hardly looking forward to facing him today, let
alone asking him anything, even a question as
simple as that. She had finally decided at

about four in the morning that her best
approach if she wanted to keep her sanity and,
more important, her job, was just to cool it
with him. This body language had driven her
crazy last night as she'd tried to analyze every
little movement she'd made in front of Jeff the
day before. She wasn't about to go through
that again.

"Okay, but don't think I'll forget," Russ
warned.

That, Leslie thought, she could count on.
She heard Russ retreat to his room and went
back to her task. She sorely needed some
work on her face, she thought, but after only
two hours of deep sleep, this seemed pretty
difficult to do just now. She splashed her face
with cold water several times to wake up, but
even this had little effect, so she decided to
give it up. Right now it was black coffee time,
and she smelled some brewing downstairs.

"Good morning, Leslie. You're looking
pretty as always," Jed said when she entered
the kitchen.

Leslie knew better than to fall for Jed's
flattery. Unfortunately, she knew that the bags
under her eyes did not make a pretty sight.

"Flattery will get you nowhere, but pouring
me a cup of coffee might work," she said. Jed
was such a softie—Leslie knew that he would

do anything for her. Usually, she hated to take advantage of him, but this morning she was desperate. And it felt good to know that at least one guy found her attractive, although she didn't really take Jed's crush seriously.

She sat down at the dining room table while Jed brought her a mug of coffee. She slugged down half of it before she set the mug down.

"Oh, that's better. I can open one eye. Thanks a bunch, Jed. Why is the table set?" Leslie asked, noticing the six place settings around the table.

"Pamela's leaving today. So Russ and I decided last night to make her a send-off breakfast."

"Pamela's leaving?" Leslie said in surprise.

"She's not really leaving," Russ replied, appearing from upstairs. "She's just going home for a little while."

"Why is she going home?"

"I'm not too sure," Russ answered. "But she said she'll be back in a week or two."

"Well, if it's a send-off breakfast for Pamela, where's the guest of honor?"

"She'll probably be down any minute. Jed, have you got the pancakes under control? I've got to put up some bacon."

"Aye, aye, captain," Jed answered.

Why is Russ going to so much trouble for

Pamela? Leslie wondered as she watched him tend to the sizzling bacon. *I didn't think he even liked her.* As for Leslie, she didn't know Pamela very well, but she sure did admire her wardrobe.

Sure enough, just when breakfast was ready, Pamela came down looking elegant as ever in a suede miniskirt, matching suede shoes and shoulder bag, an ivory-colored silk blouse, and classy gold jewelry. Then Tracy and Fury joined everyone at the table, looking fresh as daisies after their late night, in twin "Original Party Animal" T-shirts.

"Hot off the griddle," Jed shouted as he brought over a stack of pancakes. Russ followed with plenty of bacon for everyone. No sooner were the platters of food passed around the table than refills were already in order. Fortunately, Russ and Jed had seconds warming in the oven.

In spite of the fact that Russ and Jed had prepared the breakfast especially for her, Pamela limited her morning intake to her usual two cups of coffee and one glass of orange juice. Her conversation was equally sparse.

Leslie couldn't stand her silence and finally asked her, "Why are you going home, Pamela?"

"Oh, just some family business to take care of. I'll be back soon."

Leslie had to be content with Pamela's cryptic answer, as it appeared that she wasn't going to say anymore. Leslie wasn't even sure Pamela would be courteous enough to acknowledge Russ and Jed for their efforts on her behalf. "Thank you, Russ. Thank you, Jed, for a delicious breakfast," Pamela said at last. "It was very sweet of you to make it for me."

Not that she's eating any of it, Leslie thought.

"Yeah, thanks, guys. That was great," Fury agreed, polishing off the last of the pancakes.

"Let us help clear," Tracy said, talking for herself and her boyfriend.

"I hate to eat and run," Leslie apologized, "but I've got to get to work. Thanks again, guys. Let's do this again sometime. Are you coming with me, Fury?"

"Tracy's opening up the store. I'll catch a ride with her. Thanks, anyway."

"I'll ride in with you," Russ suggested to Leslie. "If you feel up to it, maybe we can go out to eat when you get off work. My treat."

Leslie had a feeling she should be suspicious of her brother's motives, but he seemed to be genuinely nice this morning. "If I'm not too tired, that sounds like a great idea. Thanks, Russ."

"In that case I need to run upstairs and get a change of clothes. I'll just be a minute."

"Me, too. I'll meet you at the car," Leslie said, heading up to her bedroom to finish dressing. Already in her aqua and pink racing Arena and pink running shorts, all she had to do was slip into her aqua Keds and her lifeguard sweatshirt. Her beach bag with all her other lifeguard paraphernalia was in the car. She grabbed her car keys from off the night table, and a pair of white pants with a striped top from the closet, and flew out of the house. Russ was right behind her.

"I'll drive," he said as they rounded the corner of the house and came into the carport. Leslie hesitated long enough to stuff her change of clothes into her beach bag on the backseat, then handed him the keys. It had been a while since he'd driven the car, she reasoned, so it's only fair.

"I hope there aren't any banana peels in the garage," she said, referring to the bizarre way Russ had cracked up their brand new Suzuki at the beginning of the summer. To this day Leslie had trouble believing how the accident had happened. As Russ had more than once explained it to her, he was parking the jeep when he aimed a banana peel into a nearby trash can, but it had fallen into the road, where Chris, his volleyball buddy, had slipped on it. Russ had swerved to miss hitting his friend, and ended up hitting a pole instead.

"No banana peels, orange peels, peels of any kind. Don't worry, Leslie, I'll be careful."

Leslie just nodded, but she wasn't really listening anymore. As soon as Russ turned onto the highway leading into town, she closed her eyes and leaned her head back. The warm sun directly on her face made her feel even sleepier. As she drifted off, she only hoped she could stay awake on the job.

Leslie was asleep for the whole ride until Russ hit the brakes, turned off the ignition, and said, "You know, Les, the car is only going to sit here all day. What harm is there in my having it while you're at work?"

Only then did she realize that they were already at the beach. And only then did she fully understand Russ's clever new approach to getting the car. Leslie didn't answer him right away, not because she was trying to be difficult, but because she was still a little drowsy. "Listen, Les," Russ continued, "I promise I'll have it back to you any time you want. Name the time."

"Okay. You win. Five o'clock sharp. I don't

want to have to wait a minute. I'll meet
you back here. Then, if I feel up to it, we
can decide where to go for dinner, okay?"
Leslie had to admit that Russ was persistent
as well as persuasive. And he was right, she
admitted to herself, she had no need for the
car during the day.

"Thanks, Leslie, you're a pal. I'll pick you up
here at five on the button. Don't forget your
bag," Russ said, taking it out of the backseat
and handing it to her.

"That's what she was, all right—a pal, a
buddy, just one of the boys," Leslie muttered
as she hopped out of the car and stepped onto
the beach. She kicked the sand in disgust and
was sorry she had done it. Now she had sand
in her sneakers. She took them off and threw
them, sand and all, into her canvas bag.
Looking down at her bare feet, she watched
the fine grains of sand sift through her toes as
she set out for her lifeguard station. The sand
was warming up quickly, she noted; it was
going to be another hot day.

Leslie was only a few feet away from the
station when—wham! The next thing she
knew she walked right into somebody.

"Hey, why don't you look where you're
going?" he said to her in a gruff voice.

Leslie looked up. It was Jeff, of all people.

She didn't know what to say. She was so confused about him as it was, and now, to make matters worse, he seemed annoyed by the little accident.

"Oh, I'm sorry. It's been one of those days," Leslie blurted out.

"Already? It's still early in the morning. Anyway," Jeff went on, "I was hoping to run into you on my way to get some coffee. I did a pretty good job of it, don't you think?"

Only now did Leslie realize that Jeff had been putting her on with his mock angry voice and had bumped into her on purpose. But for the moment that was as much as she could figure out.

Jeff leaned against the lifeguard stand and watched as Leslie went through her morning routine to prepare for the day. His steady gaze made her so nervous she squirted out way too much suntan lotion, and had to wipe the excess on her sweatshirt.

"So, what are you doing tonight?" he asked casually.

"Russ is picking me up at five o'clock. If I'm not too tired, we might go out to dinner. Otherwise, we'll probably go straight home," Leslie answered. *Does he want me to work tonight or something?* she wondered. *Maybe there's some special event on the beach tonight that I haven't heard about.*

"That's a good idea. Let's go out to eat tonight. Why don't you tell Russ to go home without you?"

"Then how will I get home?"

"I'll drive you. Hello," Jeff said, playfully knocking her on the head. "Anybody home in there?"

"Oh, of course, you'll drive me. Thanks. I mean, that works out great. Then Russ can have the car tonight. I think he'll go for that idea."

How dumb could she get? she wondered now, mentally hitting herself on the head. *Jeff was asking her for a date!*

"So, what would you like to eat? Mexican? Chinese? Seafood?"

Jeff is asking me for a date! Leslie thought. *I can't believe it. I wonder if my body language worked after all. Or maybe he had the same dream I had last night about the two of us on the beach. What difference does it make why? He really asked me out—that's what counts!* Leslie was so happy she felt like laughing out loud.

"So, what'll it be?" Jeff was saying.

"Hmm? What'll what be?" she asked, her thoughts returning to the moment.

Jeff gave her a curious look. "Dinner. What do you want to eat? Is seafood okay?"

"Oh sure. I love seafood."

"Great. Let's try Port of Call on the pier. I'd better make a reservation. It gets pretty crowded around dinner time. I may not be able to see you on patrol later, so let's decide when and where we should meet," Jeff suggested.

Leslie's brain was working normally now. "Why don't we meet at the Surfrider Cafe, say around five-thirty? That'll give me time to tell Russ what's happening and to change."

"We've got a date. See you at five-thirty," Jeff said, then headed across the street to the cafe.

Chapter 5

"We've got a date! We've got a date!" Leslie shrieked as she raced into T-Shirts For Two on her lunch break.

Only one customer was in the shop. She must have been about seventy, but she certainly didn't dress her age. The woman was wearing a Marina Bay Beach Bum T-shirt, violet shorts, and running shoes to match. She looked up from the Make Pizza Not War T-shirt she was inspecting and said, "How nice for you. What's the lucky boy's name?"

"Jeff." Before Leslie had a chance to share any more information, Tracy came out from the back of the store with some more T-shirts for her friendly customer.

"Well, hi there, Leslie. I'll be with you in a minute," Tracy said. She turned to the woman. "What do you think of this one, Mrs. Owen? This Surf Mars T-shirt is different. You don't see that one on everybody."

"That's very nice, but I just don't know. What about that cute one with the dinosaur wearing flowered shorts and holding a beach umbrella?" Mrs. Owen said, pointing to another shirt high up on the wall.

"You mean Beachasaurus." Tracy reached into a drawer behind the counter and came up with the Beachasaurus decal to show Mrs. Owen. "Here it is. This one's real popular."

Leslie watched her friend help Mrs. Owen and marveled at her patience. At the moment, patience was definitely not one of her own virtues. *When will Mrs. Owen make up her mind?* Leslie wondered, feeling as if she couldn't contain her news another minute. *I can't wait here all day.* She had just about decided to go get some lunch first, then come back to see Tracy, when at last Mrs. Owen said, "Oh, that is adorable. I'll take one in a medium size."

Tracy walked to the back to get her the shirt.

"What did you say is the name of the boy you're going out with?" Mrs. Owen asked, picking up the conversation she had started with Leslie exactly where she had left off.

"Jeff."

"And I bet Jeff is quite a good-looker."

"Yes." What was taking Tracy so long? Leslie was feeling very frustrated. She'd end up telling Mrs. Owen instead of her roommate all about her date with Jeff tonight.

"You two must make a lovely couple. You're quite pretty yourself."

"Thank you." Leslie appreciated the woman's compliment, but she would have appreciated Tracy's return even more. *That's it, I can't wait any longer,* Leslie thought, but then Tracy finally came out from the back.

"I'm terribly sorry, Mrs. Owen. We're out of mediums, so I brought you a large instead," she said to her customer.

"I just don't know. Do they shrink?" Mrs. Owen asked.

"Not really," Tracy said honestly. "But all the girls like to wear them big."

"Sorry to interrupt, but I've got to go," Leslie said abruptly. If she lingered any longer, she'd have no time to eat her lunch.

"Don't go. I'm almost done," Tracy whispered.

"I like my shirts roomy, too. I'll take it." Mrs. Owen reached into her purse for her money.

Quickly Tracy rang up the transaction and bagged the shirt. "Here you go. Wear it in good health," she told Mrs. Owen with a smile.

Leslie and Tracy waited quietly while Mrs. Owen made her way to the exit, stopping every so often to look at another shirt.

"Now what did you want to tell me?" Tracy asked as soon as the door had shut behind Mrs. Owen.

"Tracy, he asked me out."

"Who, Leslie? Who asked you out?"

"Jeff. Who do you think?"

"How am I supposed to know? As of yesterday, except in your dreams, I thought he wasn't in the picture. How did it happen?"

"Well, this morning as I was on my way to my tower I ran into Jeff. I think he was waiting for me to show up. Anyway, then and there he asked me out. Oh, Tracy, I'm so happy I could die. He's taking me out for dinner tonight."

"Before you die, tell where he's taking you."

"To Port of Call—you know, that fancy place on the pier. I hope Jeff's prepared for an expensive date. Now that I don't have time for lunch, I'll probably be starving by the time we go out for dinner."

"Leslie, that's wonderful. Maybe the four of

us can double-date sometime," Tracy suggested.

"If Jeff and I make it through this date, that sounds like a great idea." Leslie glanced at her Swatch. "Oh, my God, it's a quarter to one. I've really got to go. I'll talk to you tonight. If you're up when I get home, that is," Leslie said, winking at Tracy.

"Have a great time tonight. Don't do anything I wouldn't do."

"Thanks, Tracy. That leaves me plenty of leeway."

"Why not? Girls just want to have fun," her roommate sang.

"And this girl's planning on having some, that's for sure," Leslie said, and practically danced out of the store.

After her lunch break it was harder than ever for Leslie to keep her mind on the job. When she wasn't daydreaming about Jeff, she was thinking about food. Finally, she was so hungry that she even ate the slightly sandy, stale piece of toast that was still in her bag from yesterday.

Tracy had been right when she had said to her last night that she had it bad. Every gorgeous hunk parading on the beach reminded her of Jeff, except that he was better looking. She checked her Swatch nearly every five minutes, thinking that it was five minutes closer to their date. It was a good thing Jeff had only asked her that morning—if he'd asked more than a day in advance, she didn't think her nerves would have survived. As it was, that last hour before she went off duty seemed as long as the rest of the entire day. She had to concentrate extra hard to stay alert. Luckily for Leslie, when the sky clouded over in the late afternoon, all except the most hardy beachgoers packed up their boom boxes and beach gear and went home, making it easier for her to keep tabs on the few diehards still in the water.

By the time five o'clock rolled around, she was out of her mind with anticipation. She grabbed her beach bag, bounded down from her lifeguard station and raced across the sand to the volleyball courts, where Russ had dropped her off that morning. The Surfrider Cafe was just across the street and about half a block down.

"Hi, Leslie," he called to her as she approached the jeep. "Here I am. Right on time."

Leslie walked up to the car and glanced at her Swatch. It was five past five. "Good," she said. "Just for that I'll give you a surprise."

"What kind of surprise? You're treating me to dinner?"

"Something even better than that, my dear brother."

"I can have the car tonight?"

"You guessed it."

"You're kidding. That's great!" Russ exclaimed, his eyes lighting up. "How come?"

"I'm going out to dinner with Jeff," Leslie said coolly, as if she went out with him every night of the week.

"Well, well, well. What do you know? My little sister has a big date with the big buff," Russ said. "I'm glad Jeff finally realized what he was missing."

Leslie grinned. "Thanks."

"I mean, he couldn't do much better, could he?" Russ continued. "You've got it all, Les. Brains, beauty, brawn. Just like your brother."

"God forbid," Leslie replied in mock horror. She knew that in his inimitable way Russ was trying to give her a compliment. At the barbeque last week she had told him how she felt about Jeff. Even though Russ was her brother, Leslie had been embarrassed to talk to him about such a personal problem, but he really seemed to understand. Sometimes he wasn't such a pain in the neck after all.

"Have a great time tonight," Russ was saying now.

"Thanks." Leslie glanced at her Swatch.

Twenty minutes before her date. "I've got to run."

Leslie dashed across the street to the side of Surfrider Drive lined with stores. She raced past The Flotsam and Jetsamwich Soda Shop, Beach Boys and Girls Accessories, Tortilla Flats, The Deli, and into the Surfrider Cafe. The volleyball crowd was gathering. Leslie guessed the clouds had brought them in early. She spotted Russ's volleyball friends having a bite to eat at a table under a hanging fern in the corner. Chris looked like he was having a great time sitting between two pretty girls named Erica and Maggie. Leslie smiled—Chris was such a character. With his dark curly hair and shy grin, he reminded her of a big teddy bear. She waved to them, then headed to the ladies' room to change.

By the time she'd come out again she anticipated another change. She figured Russ would have joined them by then and the whole world would know that she was going out with Jeff. *So what?* she decided. Even if he never asked her out again, she had a date with him tonight, and that was something worth shouting about. *Besides, when Jeff shows up to meet me, they'll all find out anyway. It's not as if I have anything to hide. I just don't want to get any guff, or I know I'll lose my cool,* she concluded, stepping into a bathroom stall to change.

As she slipped out of her shorts and tank suit, she imagined she was Superwoman changing into her street clothes. *But I don't think being a lifeguard is in quite the same league as Superwoman. And if there were a Superwoman, she'd certainly change into something a heck of a lot nicer than this to go on the hottest date of her life,* Leslie thought looking down at the white pants and aqua-and-white striped jersey and matching aqua Keds that she had stuffed into her beach bag that morning when she thought she'd be going out to dinner with Russ. She made a quick stop at the mirror to run a brush through her hair and put on a splash of makeup and lipstick. One last glimpse of herself and she had to admit that for a quick-change artist she looked pretty good. Even those bags under her eyes seemed to have disappeared since the morning. *I hope Jeff will think I look good,* she thought.

She came out of the bathroom and looked around for Jeff. She soon spotted him through the crowd, wearing a plaid sport shirt, soft blue sweater, and a pair of gray Bugle Boys, talking to Russ and his friends. Leslie's heart raced as she walked over to him. His muscles swelled just beneath the surface of his clothes, and he looked even better than he usually did in only a bathing suit. As she approached him, Leslie couldn't help but notice how his sweater brought out the blue in his eyes. "Slow down," she said to her heart, "or you'll have a massive heart attack before the night is over."

Leslie took a deep breath. "Hi, everyone," she said. "Hi, Jeff. I'm glad I found you. It's pretty crowded in here."

"No problem. I knew I'd find you. I just looked for the foxiest chick in the cafe," Jeff said.

"Whew!" Chris said, "This is getting heavy already."

At first Leslie didn't know how to take the compliment. But she wasn't going to stand there in front of everybody and just blush. She was determined to act more adult and self-assured than that, more like the kind of woman that would attract a guy like Jeff in the first place. "Thanks, Jeff. That was sweet. Now let's go eat. I'm starving. I haven't eaten all day."

"Where are you two heading?" Russ asked.

"We've got a reservation at Ports of Call," Jeff replied.

"Well, just remember, that's my sister you're going out with," Russ reminded him as Leslie and Jeff made their way past the old surfboards mounted on the walls, and the potted plants hanging down from the ceiling. As they reached the door, Jeff slipped his arm around Leslie's waist.

For a moment Leslie tensed, then she relaxed. She liked the feel of Jeff's arm around her. It made her feel special and secure. As they strolled down the pier toward the restaurant, she noticed several girls' heads turn. From the way the girls looked at the two of them together, she knew that she wasn't the only one who thought they made a dynamite couple.

Chapter 6

"This way please," the maitre d' said to Jeff and Leslie as he escorted them to their table.

Jeff must have gone to considerable trouble to get this table, Leslie thought as the maitre d' seated her next to a window overlooking the water. Jeff sat down across from her and the maitre d' handed them their menus.

"Your waiter will be right with you," he told them. "Have a nice dinner."

Leslie looked around the restaurant before opening the menu. The new "in" spot on the pier was done in natural pine with forest-green tablecloths, peach napkins, and brass lamps on all the tables. Decorating the walls were symbols of the sea—portholes, anchors, ropes, nets, and shells. There was even a dance floor and a video being shown on a big screen in the bar.

But the restaurant's best feature as far as Leslie was concerned was the expansive window with its view of the sky and the ocean. Leslie gazed through the glass at the scene outside. She could see that the sun was making a feeble attempt to peek out from behind the clouds to no avail. Small craft were lowering their sails and calling it a day. Scavenger sea gulls followed the fishing boats as they came into port, just for a taste of the discards from their day's catch. This was a side of Marina Bay that she rarely saw. She glanced back at Jeff and found him looking at her with a smile.

"Nice, isn't it?" he asked. "I was glad when you said you liked seafood so we could come here."

"It's a great place," Leslie agreed.

The look in Jeff's eyes was making her pulse race. She took several controlled breaths as she tried to think of something else to say. *Leslie Stevens, you'd better pull yourself together or Jeff is going to think you're a real idiot*, she told herself sternly. She reached over to pick up her water glass, but as she put her hand out, she knocked her knife and fork to the floor.

"Oh, no," she cried. "I'm such a klutz. I'm so sorry," she said to the waiter who immediately appeared to give her a new set of silverware.

Leslie could feel the heat rushing to her cheeks. She knew she was making a big deal of nothing, but now that her nerves had surfaced, she couldn't seem to calm herself.

"I can't believe I did that. And in such a nice restaurant, too," she babbled on. "I guess you just can't take me anywhere, I'm such a klutz."

Jeff covered her hand lightly with both of his. "Relax," he said with an amused smile. "You're not a klutz. If you were, you wouldn't be such a terrific lifeguard. Besides, all you did was drop your silverware. It's not such a catastrophe."

Leslie ventured a glance across the table and caught Jeff's eye. She couldn't help but grin. He was right—she was being ridiculous.

"Now let's relax and have a good time, okay?" Jeff said, giving her hand a squeeze.

For the rest of the evening, Leslie followed his advice. At times it was still difficult to think of things to talk about other than work, but the silences were not so uncomfortable, and Leslie began to enjoy simply basking in the warmth of Jeff's gaze.

"A toast to our first date," Jeff said, picking up his glass.

This time Leslie was very careful as she reached over to pick up her own glass.

"May this date be the first of many more," Jeff declared, clinking glasses.

Leslie's heart fluttered. She couldn't believe her wish was coming true.

It was dark outside by the time they had finished dinner. As they stepped into the night air, Leslie could feel the drop in temperature. She wished she had something else with her besides her oversized sweatshirt. Jeff took her hand as they started walking down the pier toward his car.

"It's still early. Want to go for a drive?" he asked.

Leslie hesitated. She wasn't so naive that she didn't know that going for a drive really meant parking and making out. *Should I or shouldn't I?* she asked herself. She thought about her conversation with Tracy earlier. Sure, she wanted to have fun, but she wasn't certain of how much and how soon.

"How about going dancing?" she suggested, avoiding a straight answer. She hoped he wouldn't be too disappointed.

To her relief, his eyes lit up. "Why don't we just go back inside the restaurant? The music sounded pretty good."

"I'm up for it," she said enthusiastically.

They walked back into the bar, where the band was playing a fast song.

"C'mon, let's dance," Jeff said.

Leslie whipped off her bulky sweatshirt and followed Jeff onto the dance floor. She knew she'd be sweating inside her sweatshirt if she'd kept it on. Her jersey was much more comfortable for dancing.

For the next couple of hours, Leslie and Jeff kept up with the fast beat of the band. Leslie's favorite songs, though, were the slow ones, when she could rest her head against Jeff's shoulder and inhale the spicy scent of his aftershave.

"Let's cut out. It's getting crowded," Jeff suggested after they'd stopped for a break.

Leslie slipped back into her sweatshirt. On the way out she took one last look around the bar and restaurant. She wanted to remember this place and this night forever.

"I had a really nice evening," Jeff said, once they had reached his car. "But I guess it has to end sometime. We both have to work early tomorrow."

Leslie wondered for a fleeting moment if

he'd been reading her mind. "I guess you're right," she said softly.

"The weather's turned lousy, anyway," Jeff went on. "Maybe it'll be a nicer evening tomorrow. Why don't we pick up tomorrow where we left off tonight?" he asked.

Leslie wasn't exactly sure what Jeff meant by this last question, but there was only one way to find out. "Sure," she said, "I'd like that."

Chapter 7

Leslie opened the front door. All the lights were off downstairs. She flicked on the hall light and tiptoed upstairs.

"Why are you back so early? It's only eleven o'clock," Russ asked, peering out from his bedroom as she passed by. "Didn't you have a good time?"

"I had a great time," Leslie replied, but she didn't stop to add more.

"Aren't you going to tell us about it?" Jed asked, joining Russ at the doorway.

"Nope."

"Come on, Leslie, humor us," Jed pleaded.

"You may not believe this, but it's been so long since I had a date, I've forgotten what it's like."

Leslie heard her brother add something, but she continued on down the hall to her bedroom in search of Tracy. Leslie had seen her roommate's Honda 500 parked in the carport when she peeked in to see if her own baby, her Suzuki, had made it back safely. Her jeep and Tracy were home, thank goodness.

She couldn't wait to tell Tracy all about her evening. But that, Leslie discovered as soon as she walked into the room, would take a little doing. Her roommate had konked out on her bed with all the lights and her clothes on. Leslie might have felt guilty about waking her up, but she knew Tracy would want to get undressed before going to sleep for the night.

"I'm up. I'm up," her roommate said sleepily, as Leslie shook her gently. "So, how did your date go, Les?"

"Oh, Tracy. Words can't describe it." Leslie kicked off her Keds and stretched out on her bed.

"You woke me up to tell me this? Unless you plan to draw me a picture, you'll have to use a few descriptive adjectives."

"Oh, Tracy, all I can say is . . ." Leslie stopped talking in mid-sentence, lost in her own thoughts.

"I know. All you can say is 'Oh, Tracy.' I'm going back to sleep."

"Tracy, no. Don't go back to sleep. I have so much to tell you."

"Then you'd better start talking. I don't have all night. I need my beauty sleep."

"Oh, Tracy . . ."

"I've heard that before."

"Jeff is so wonderful. He got us a table by the window, where we could see the harbor," she began. "He toasted our first date together and said he hoped it would be the first of many. I never thought he would be so romantic."

"Now you're talking," Tracy said. "What did you do after dinner? Tell me *everything*."

Leslie knew exactly what Tracy meant by "everything", but in all honesty, there wasn't much of "everything" to tell. She hesitated. All of a sudden she felt funny telling that to Tracy. "Well, uh, Jeff wanted to go for a drive, but I thought we'd better not, at least not on our first date."

"Wise move," Tracy said, to her roommate's surprised relief. "You've got plenty of time together if you want to get that serious." Tracy got up and started undressing. "So if you didn't go for a drive, what did you do?"

"We went dancing." Leslie let out a deep

sigh. "Oh, Tracy, Jeff's a great dancer. But that's not even the best part. He asked me out for tomorrow night."

"Leslie, that's great! If all goes well tomorrow, why don't we double-date Saturday night?" Tracy suggested. "We can all go to the Fun Zone. I want to try that Big Wave roller coaster I've heard about."

"That sounds terrific. But I'll have to check with Jeff. I'll let you know if he's up for it."

"Okay," Tracy replied. "So tell me what else happened tonight? Did he kiss you?"

Leslie blushed, remembering once more the tender kiss. She touched her lips, felt a tingle run through her body, and completely forgot she was talking to Tracy.

"Come in, Leslie. This is earth to Leslie. Do you read me? Over and out."

"Huh?" Leslie replied, startled out of her reverie.

"Well, I guess that answers my question," Tracy said with a grin.

Leslie blushed even pinker. "The answer to your question is yes, he kissed me good night."

"Must've been good," Tracy teased. "It seems like you've fallen head over heels after just the one kiss. You and Sleeping Beauty. Talking about girls that like to sleep, I wouldn't mind some more myself. Now can I get undressed?"

"Oh, sure. I hope you didn't mind my waking you. But I just had to talk to you."

"No problem, Leslie. I wanted to hear all about your date. I'm really happy for you. Now I'm looking forward to tomorrow night's installment."

"That makes two of us."

Tracy got up and put on her nightie while Leslie lay on her bed in a trance, already imagining the next episode. Would they end up taking a drive tomorrow night? Leslie pictured herself in Jeff's arms. She could almost feel his tender kisses.

Heaven, she thought. *What a perfect way to spend an evening. Why on earth did I say I didn't want to go for a drive tonight? We could have kissed all night instead of just once at the door.* She sighed contentedly. *Oh well, I had a fantastic evening anyway. Besides, there's always tomorrow to go for a drive.* The thought gave her a warm feeling inside. *Just don't get too carried away,* she warned herself sternly.

Chapter 8

If Russ had asked Leslie for the jeep on Wednesday morning, she would have given it to him no questions asked. What need did she have for worldly possessions now that she was going out with Jeff? As for getting to work, it would have been an excuse to drive in with Jeff. On the other hand, she could have flown there, she felt so high. But Russ wasn't up in time to ask anyway, for it was only six-thirty when Leslie leaped out of bed, already a ball of energy at that early hour.

On most mornings it took Leslie several minutes to decide what to wear, but this morning she immediately decided on her yellow tank suit and gear in keeping with her sunny mood. She quietly dressed and packed up for the day, careful not to awaken Tracy.

She glanced out the bedroom window toward the ocean; it looked like the day was going to suit her mood. The sun had just come up and the sky was already clear. Picking up her beach bag, she headed downstairs in plenty of time to fix herself a good breakfast.

"Well, good morning. Look who's up at the crack of dawn," Jed greeted her.

"Look who's talking. What gets you up so early?" Leslie asked. She wasn't at all surprised to find Jed engaged in his favorite activity in his favorite room—that is, eating in the kitchen—but what did surprise her was the time of day. Jed didn't usually get down to the kitchen until around eight-thirty in the morning.

"I'm taking Alex out on a fishing boat this morning. We have to be at the pier by eight o'clock."

Alex, Leslie knew, was the seven-year-old kid Jed was taking care of this summer. She also knew that taking Alex anywhere was like taking your life in your hands. Jed deserved a lot of credit for having the guts to take Alex fishing. *I hope Alex doesn't try the same trick on Jed that he tried on Russ*, she thought, remembering the day that Jed had asked her brother to look after his charge. Russ had planned to take Alex fishing, but before he'd even had a chance to rent the boat and tackle, the little brat had run away and fallen off the edge of the pier. Fortunately, Fury and his friends had been surfing in the area and had come to the rescue.

"I hope you're bringing a restraint harness for Alex," Leslie commented now.

"Very funny, Leslie," Jed replied. "I am prepared for anything."

As usual, Leslie remarked to herself. Jed was dressed just like a professional fisherman, from his blue woolen cap to his high rubber boots. No matter what the sport, she could count on Jed to be properly outfitted—even if he'd never tried the sport before.

"You're in an exceptionally good mood for this time of day," Jed continued. "How come?"

Leslie wasn't sure how to answer Jed's question. From his behavior the night before, he obviously knew that she'd had a date. Perhaps he was trying another way to get information? Maybe he was still hoping that he had a chance with her. *Most likely it's just an innocent question*, she told herself. *Jed is just making conversation.*

"Woke up on the right side of the bed, I guess," she said finally. She gave him a casual smile that she hoped hid the real reason for her good mood.

"I've already made the coffee. Can I pour you a cup?" Jed asked, getting up from his chair with his cup in hand.

"Sure, thanks, Jed," she replied gratefully.

As she sipped the coffee Jed had poured for her, Leslie got busy in the kitchen making herself some eggs and toast. Jed went back to finishing his breakfast. When he was done, he cleared away his dishes, grabbed a yellow slicker from off the back of his chair, and said, "Gotta go. See you later, Leslie."

"Good luck fishing. Hope you catch a big one, and I don't mean Alex," Leslie shouted as Jed headed out of the house.

She settled back to enjoy a leisurely breakfast with only her thoughts as company. The main subject on her mind, of course, was Jeff. Although she'd been eyeing him since the beginning of the summer, it seemed now as if their relationship had begun suddenly.

I wonder why it took him so long to ask me out? He certainly had plenty of chances when we were driving to work together, she mused. *I guess Jeff just realized his feelings yesterday morning . . .* but then Leslie recalled his odd behavior on Monday, when he'd said that he missed her already as she left for her afternoon break. *But then why did he seem so annoyed when I came back? Could he be shy?* Leslie grinned at the thought. *How could Jeff be shy? He's got millions of girls chasing him.* Dreamily she ate the last of her eggs. *And he chose me!*

Still thinking of the head lifeguard, Leslie glanced at her Swatch. It had somehow gotten late. *Uh oh, I can't be late to work*, she thought, as she quickly put her plate in the dishwasher. *That wouldn't make a very good impression.*

"You'll be needing these," Russ said, coming downstairs as Leslie was on her way out. He handed her the car keys.

Leslie took them gratefully. "Thanks, Russ. I guess I wouldn't have gotten too far without the keys."

"Thanks for the car," Russ replied.

"That's okay. Look, Russ, I'm in a hurry. I don't know if I'll be home for dinner or not so don't plan on me."

"Then you had a good time last night and it's more of the same tonight, huh?"

"Something like that. Gotta go."

Leslie had one foot out the door when Fury

shouted from the den, "Hey, wait for me. I'll be out in a minute."

There was something nice about having a routine in the morning, Leslie thought, as she backed the jeep out of the carport and let it idle in the street as she waited for Fury, as usual.

He hopped in the car with only one high-top sneaker on and earrings in only one ear. But by the time Leslie found a parking space in town, he was wearing one sneaker on each foot, four earrings in each ear, one T-shirt, and one pair of cut-offs.

"Any messages for Tracy?" Fury asked as he got out of the car.

"Not today. I talked to her last night," Leslie said, grabbing her bag from the backseat.

"See you later then," Fury said, and headed to his tower at the other end of the beach.

Leslie made tracks to hers. She set about her morning tasks with unusual vigor. Just in case Jeff should drop by her station, she wanted to be ready. She was just applying some suntan oil when she noticed a man staggering down the otherwise deserted sand. As he came closer, Leslie could tell that he had most probably spent the night on the beach. *Didn't he notice all the signs saying that it's against the law?* she wondered. She took a closer look at him. *On second thought, he doesn't look as if he cares. This must be the drifter Fury mentioned the other day.* The drifter's face was unshaven, and his jeans dirty and torn. His sun-bleached hair was straggly, with bits of sand clinging to it, and he carried a ragged old sleeping bag slung over his shoulder.

"Rapunzel, Rapunzel, let down your long blond hair," he shouted up to her.

Leslie was really annoyed. Just when she had made up her mind to be more open, now she had to do her best to ignore the drifter. She hoped that if she paid no attention to him, he would just move along. She didn't want to have to use her authority with him. But the bum wouldn't take the hint.

"Rapunzel, Rapunzel, let down your long blond hair so I may climb up to your tower." This time he sounded more insistent.

Leslie continued to ignore him, hoping he would go away.

"If you don't let down your hair, I'm coming up there and dragging you down," the bum yelled, and without waiting he dropped his sleeping bag in the sand and swung himself up onto the crossbar of the lifeguard stand.

For a moment Leslie sat rooted to the spot, the bottle of suntan oil still in her hand. She saw the drifter's hands appear above the edge of the platform, then his bloodshot eyes.

All right. You asked for it, mister, she thought, springing into action. She reached down and squirted the lotion at his hands.

"Hey!" the drifter yelled in surprise as he lost his grip and fell backward into the sand.

Leslie had thought that would be the end of him and he'd leave her alone, but she couldn't have been more wrong. Her action had only infuriated him further.

"You'll be sorry you did that, little girl!" he yelled.

The next thing she knew, the lifeguard stand was trembling so violently, Leslie thought it was going to topple over. She caught a glimpse of the drifter's menacing face looking up at her as he shook one of the wooden legs of the tower, and she knew that was exactly what he wanted. Her stomach tightened with fear.

"Rapunzel, Rapunzel, I said let down your long blond hair," he repeated angrily, "or your tower is gonna come crashing down!"

Leslie held her breath and jumped. Although it was only about six feet to the ground, it seemed like miles before she landed. Her feet touched down first, but she couldn't keep her balance in the slippery sand and she ended up on her rear.

"Rapunzel, you've let down your hair," said a threatening voice from behind her.

Leslie didn't hesitate. She spun around quickly, kicking sand in the drifter's face. He took a step back in surprise, giving Leslie a chance to get back on her feet. Suddenly two strong hands appeared to help her up.

"Are you okay?" Jeff asked.

The drifter had obviously had enough. He took the opportunity to run. But Jeff was right behind him, and in no time he'd tackled the drifter in the sand. Leslie watched in horror as Jeff raised his fist.

"You low-down creep. If you want to rough someone up, why not try me?" Jeff said. He stood up, leaving the drifter lying in the sand. "What's the matter? You afraid?" he taunted.

He reached down and lifted the drifter up by the sleeve of his well-worn T-shirt. The drifter squirmed, but Jeff held tight.

"I think we'd better call the police, Leslie," he went on.

At the mention of the police, Leslie noticed a look of panic appear in the drifter's eyes.

"No police," he begged.

But Jeff had already taken his walkie-talkie from his belt. "Trouble at tower four. Dispatch patrol car immediately."

The drifter obviously wasn't going to wait

around. While Jeff's attention was sidetracked by the walkie-talkie, he yanked his shirt away and raced up the beach toward the street. This time Jeff didn't follow.

He turned to Leslie. "Good thing I came by when I did. He got really scared when I brought out this handy little walkie-talkie, but I didn't even turn it on. I just wanted to scare him." He looked at Leslie in concern. "Are you all right?"

Leslie brushed the sand off her tank suit and said, "I'm okay. Just a little shook up, that's all."

Jeff put his arm around her to comfort her. "Why don't you take the rest of the day off? I'll cover your tower."

"Really, Jeff. I'm okay now." With Jeff's arm around her, she was feeling much better. "That guy was a real nut. Maybe we should have called the police for real. I don't like the thought of him doing that again."

"I don't think he'd dare," Jeff said. "But if he does come around here again, I won't hesitate to call the police." He looked at her with concern. "Are you sure you're okay? The more I think about it, the more I feel I wouldn't be doing my job if I didn't tell you to take the rest of the day off. I'll pick you up after dinner, say around seven-thirty. By then you'll have gotten over this whole horrible incident."

"Jeff, I'm fine now," Leslie insisted. "The beach is going to start filling up soon, so it will be just like any other day at work."

"I don't know, Les, I really think you ought to go home. That isn't a request—that's an order from your boss," Jeff said with a grin.

Leslie knew he was only teasing, but still she resented the way he was confusing his role as her new boyfriend with that of her boss. She was glad he'd shown up when he did, but she didn't like the way he just took over. He was treating her like a helpless female and she didn't like it. Hadn't she just proved that she wasn't helpless?

"Come on, I'll walk you to your car," Jeff continued, obviously unaware of the thoughts going through Leslie's mind.

"All right, I'll go home," she conceded. *Actually, I wouldn't mind taking the rest of the day off, but I can certainly walk to the car on my own*, she added to herself. "You stay here and man the tower," she said to Jeff. "See you at seven-thirty." With that, Leslie gathered her things into her beach bag and headed toward the jeep.

Chapter 9

"You're home early. Must have been a rough day, huh?" Russ remarked when Leslie arrived home.

"You could say that," she said. She trudged straight into the living room, slipped out of her sneakers, dropped her beach bag on the floor and herself onto one of the peach-colored sofas. Russ followed her in and sank into the other sofa.

"Anyone home?" Leslie asked.

"No, I'm the only one here."

"Oh," Leslie replied.

Russ gave her a curious look. "So why are you home early?"

Leslie shrugged. "No reason."

"There has to be a reason," Russ declared. "What happened? Did they close the beach or something? Has Jaws come to visit Marina Bay?"

"Very funny," Leslie said, but she didn't even smile.

"Les, I don't know why, but I have this feeling you're not telling me something. No more joking now," he said. "What happened?"

Leslie really didn't feel like telling Russ what had happened. Just thinking about it got her upset. At least she had been quick to defend herself. *I could have easily frozen up with fear, and then what would have happened?* The thought made her shudder.

"C'mon, Leslie," Russ persisted. "Something's happened to you and I'd like to know what."

Leslie could hear Russ's concern loud and clear. She decided he deserved a straight answer.

"Some beach bum attacked me while I was on duty," she said. She hoped she sounded calmer than she felt as she described what had happened.

"Les, are you all right? Did he hurt you?"

"Not really. Just roughed me up a little."

"I wish I'd been there," Russ said. "Nobody messes with my sister and gets away with it."

Leslie grinned. Russ was so funny when he tried to act like a macho big brother. Inside she knew he was just a big softie. *But why do I get so annoyed when Jeff acts protective?* she wondered.

"It sounds like you did a pretty good job on him yourself, Leslie," Russ continued. "I didn't know you were such a tough cookie."

"Neither did I," Leslie replied. "I didn't really think about what I was doing. I just knew that I had to get that guy away from me."

"Well, hard luck on the guys who try to mess with Leslie Stevens," Russ remarked with a grin. He glanced at his watch and stood up. "I'm supposed to meet Chris at the volleyball courts. Are you sure you're okay?"

"Yup, I'm a tough cookie, remember?" Leslie said. "Actually, I am kind of tired all of a sudden. I think I'll take a nap."

"Good idea," Russ agreed as he turned to go.

"Hey, Russ?"

He turned back around. "Yeah?"

"Thanks. I feel a lot better."

"Any time, sis. After all, what are brothers for?" he said. "See you around six."

"Wait a minute, Russ. Just one more thing," Leslie said, reaching into her beach bag. She pulled out the keys and tossed them to Russ. "I won't be needing the car today, so it's all yours."

"Thanks, Les, I'll take good care of it," Russ promised. "Now get some rest."

Leslie heard Russ go out the door, then she stretched out on the couch. She had intended to take a nap upstairs, but now she couldn't seem to find the energy to move. She closed her eyes.

The next thing she heard was someone clumping around in the kitchen, but she was too tired to get up and investigate. A moment later Jed appeared, still in his high rubber boots and blue woolen cap. In his hand, however, he held a carton of yogurt where Leslie would have expected to see a fishing rod.

She checked her Swatch for the time—three o'clock. She had slept away four hours.

"You're a lot better looking than a fish, do you know that?" Jed greeted her, plopping down on the sofa that Russ had occupied earlier.

"Thanks," Leslie replied with a sleepy smile. Jed was definitely one of a kind. "How'd your day with Alex go?"

"Wait a second. Before I answer your question, I have one for you. What are you doing home?"

This time Leslie didn't mind recounting the morning's episode. She felt detached from it now—as if it had all been a bad dream or something she had seen on TV.

"Wow, Leslie, what a story!" Jed exclaimed when she had finished. "I can't believe something like that could happen in Marina Bay. This town seems so safe."

"It is usually," Leslie assured him. "I'm sure the guy must have been on drugs. He was really deranged."

"Sounds like it," Jed agreed, shoving a heaping spoonful of yogurt into his mouth. He gestured as if to say something, but waited until he swallowed. "What would you have done if Jeff hadn't shown up when he did?"

The question caught Leslie off guard. What would she have done? "I guess my next move would have been to run down to the next lifeguard station. I probably would have kicked him first to make sure he couldn't chase me."

"You probably would have been able to outrun him anyway," Jed declared. "I think that drifter chose the wrong Rapunzel. He didn't know what he was getting into. If I ever need a bodyguard, I know who to call."

"Oh, I don't know about that," Leslie replied, but inside she was glowing from the praise. "So, tell me how your day went with Alex."

"Let's just say I'd rather not talk about it," Jed said with a look of disgust on his face.

"He was really a pain, huh?"

"Not exactly. Actually, the kid had a terrific time. He bagged a twenty-five-pound salmon all by himself and won fifty dollars in the pool for catching the biggest fish."

"Beginner's luck. Did you catch anything?"

"No."

"That's why you'd rather not talk about it," Leslie said.

"You've got it," Jed replied. "Now I'm going to go upstairs and get out of these smelly clothes."

Leslie thought she'd do the same. She got up, but decided to make a detour to the fridge, where she helped herself to a box of leftover Kentucky Fried Chicken and a piece of corn on the cob. She dashed upstairs to run the bath so that it would be ready when she finished her snack. A good hot bath would certainly make her feel better. Her appetite satisfied for the moment, Leslie sank into the tub. She could feel all her muscles relaxing as the tension flowed out of her body. Just as she was about to sink deeper into the soothing water, the phone rang.

"Leslie, it's for you," Jed called.

"Take a message. I'm in the bathtub," she called back.

A few minutes later Jed returned. "It was Jeff," he said through the bathroom door. "He hopes you're feeling better. He said he'll see you at seven-thirty. He wants you to think about what you want to do tonight."

"Thanks, Jed," Leslie said, then went back to soaking in the tub. The water was cooling down, Leslie noted, but she was too comfortable even to turn on more hot water.

Let's see, what do I want to do tonight? she asked herself. Even though Jeff had been a little overbearing earlier, Leslie was still looking forward to going out with him. She knew he had her best interests at heart, he just went about it the wrong way. *He'll simply have to learn that nobody messes with Leslie Stevens*, she thought with a determined smile.

Chapter 10

The doorbell rang at precisely seven-thirty. Leslie raced to the door and opened it. Jeff was standing on the front step with his hands behind his back and a sheepish grin on his face.

"These are for you," he said, handing her a dozen long-stem yellow roses.

"Oh, Jeff," she gasped in surprise, "they're gorgeous. Thank you."

"Even after what happened this morning, it looks like you're still in a sunny mood," Jeff remarked. "The flowers match your yellow sweater."

"You noticed."

"I notice everything about you."

Leslie tried not to blush. She hid her face in the roses, pretending to smell them. Then she turned away from Jeff and started down the hall. "Come on in. I'll need to put these in water." She got down a tall glass vase from one of the kitchen cabinets, filled it with water, and arranged the flowers in it.

"Where is everybody?" Jeff asked.

"Russ and Jed went out to dinner. And Tracy and Fury haven't come back from town yet," Leslie said. She brought the flowers into the living room. "Oh, Jeff, they're really beautiful. That was so sweet of you. Thanks," she said as she set them down on the coffee table.

"Well, I just wanted to make you feel better after this morning's incident," he explained. "It must have been a horrible experience."

Leslie shrugged. "It wasn't exactly a good way to start the day," she said. "But it's over, so let's forget about it, okay?"

"You're right," Jeff agreed. "Are you ready to go?" Leslie nodded and together they walked down the drive to his Caddy. "So, what shall we do tonight?" he asked as they settled into the soft leather seats.

Leslie wanted to suggest going out to eat

again. The Kentucky Fried Chicken had only filled her up for a little while, and she hadn't eaten any dinner. But she didn't want Jeff to think that food was her main interest—although it certainly came close.

"I don't know. Maybe go for a walk on the beach and watch the sun set," she said instead.

"Have you eaten?" Jeff asked, to Leslie's relief, as he started the engine.

"I had a late lunch but I haven't eaten dinner yet. What about you?"

"Same here. Why don't we pick up something to go on Windward Way and drive up to the bluffs to watch the sunset?"

That sounded perfect to Leslie. Since their date last night, she had been looking forward to going for a drive with Jeff. Already the thought of his kisses was making her all tingly inside. And she could tell by the balmy weather that they could expect a spectacular sunset as an added attraction.

As Jeff turned onto Surfrider Drive and picked up speed, Leslie felt a rush of warm wind through her hair and a surge of adrenaline through the rest of her body. Not that she wasn't used to the feeling; she experienced it every time she roared down Surfrider in her open Suzuki. But tonight the excitement she felt was different. Tonight she was with Jeff in his 1960 flamingo-pink Cadillac convertible. But it wasn't the car that made her feel different, it was Jeff and the special way he looked at her out of the corner of his eye as he drove.

Leslie especially loved it when Jeff slowed down to the posted fifteen-miles-per-hour speed limit when he reached the edge of town. On such a beautiful evening she expected the outdoor cafe would be packed, and her guess was right. As they rolled past, Leslie watched as heads turned. She thought she spotted Miss Popular and her snotty friend from the beach at a table by the sidewalk. She scooted closer to Jeff and rested her arm in back of his seat. *If you have him, flaunt him,* Leslie thought, and sat up proud and tall in her seat as they turned the corner and headed up Windward Way.

"So, what's your pleasure, mademoiselle? Shall we dine on take-out from that fancy French restaurant, Jacques in Zee Box?" Jeff asked as they neared fast-food row. "Or does the señorita prefer the *plata del día* from south of the border, authentically prepared as only they know how at Tacky Bell?"

"I'm kind of in the mood for the elegance of

the golden arches," Leslie told him. A basic burger appealed to her right now.

"Excellent choice," Jeff agreed.

It only took a few minutes to get their dinners from the drive-thru window. Jeff gave Leslie the food to hold, then he turned back onto the street and headed up Windward to the bluffs beyond.

He followed the road up the hill to where Windward Way turned into Windward Heights. They snaked past a row of expensive homes with million-dollar views until the houses stopped and the steep bluffs began. In winter, these bluffs were open to strong winds and turbulent waves that pounded the base of the cliffs. But in summer, the gentler onshore breezes attracted the hang gliders and the crowd that came to watch them.

Jeff opted for pulling off the road at a more remote vista point rather than in the level open space that Leslie knew was set aside for parking further on. "From here, we can see the hang gliders," he told her as he turned off the ignition. "And we'll also have a better view of the sunset."

Leslie knew that Jeff really meant that they could be alone here. She suddenly felt nervous. *What have I gotten myself into?* she wondered.

"Let's break out the fast-food feast," Jeff said.

Leslie opened the white paper bag she'd been holding and passed his order over to him. Jeff went right to work on it. But Leslie, who had been starving just moments ago, was now in no hurry to eat. *This must be the first time in my life that I've lost my appetite*, she thought wryly, *but my stomach is jumping around so much, I'd better not chance it.* She looked away from her food and over to where a hang glider was lifting off from the bluff. He soared over the ocean, blending in with the birds beyond. Leslie watched several more high-flying gliders step off from the bluffs, then turned her attention back to the bag of food in her lap. She forced herself to take one bite of her burger, then found that the rest easily followed. For the moment, her nerves seemed to have disappeared.

By the time she had polished off the last of her Coke and fries, the sun began its own disappearing act. The big orange ball in the distance got smaller and smaller as it appeared to sink into the ocean. Jeff inched closer to Leslie and put his arm around her. Suddenly Leslie's nerves returned with a vengeance. Just as he made a move to kiss her, she said quickly, "Tracy wanted to know if you and I would like to go to the Fun Zone with her and Fury on Saturday night. I told her I'd ask you and let her know."

"What a great idea! Tell her I'd love to," Jeff said. He paused and looked into Leslie's eyes. "The sun's down," he added, moving close to her again.

Leslie wondered fleetingly if that was his signal to start making out. "Look at the sky. It's turning all pink," she said. She could feel her pulse racing and her heart pounding. She didn't know why she was stalling.

"I'd rather look at you. You're prettier," Jeff said.

Leslie turned the same shade of pink as the sky.

"You're blushing," he said.

This time she didn't resist as he leaned toward her to kiss her. Tentatively, she put her arms around him and kissed him back. His kiss was even warmer and softer than she remembered. She closed her eyes and relaxed in his arms.

The next thing she knew, Jeff was whispering in her ear. "Leslie, I think we'd better go."

She looked up to see a sliver of a moon surrounded by what seemed like a million stars. "I guess you're right," she agreed.

Jeff leaned over to give her another quick

kiss. "One more for the road," he said, then turned on the ignition and headlights and drove back to town.

On the ride home, Leslie kept glancing over at Jeff. She felt as if she were in the middle of a dream, but not even her dreams were as wonderful as tonight had been.

Chapter 11

After all the excitement at work on Wednesday morning, Leslie's duties as a lifeguard on Thursday seemed pretty dull. There was little to report by lunchtime—no harassments or drownings or anything out of the ordinary. In fact, the most excitement she had all morning was breaking up a sand fight between two little boys. What kept her from being bored out of her mind was thinking about Jeff. He turned up at her station late that afternoon.

"Hi. Sorry it took so long for me to get down here," he said. "I meant to stop by this morning, but I got caught up trying to work out the schedule for Saturday. Kenny Halpern says he can't work this weekend and I've been trying to convince Fury to sub for him, but he says he wants to rest up for the Fun Zone on Saturday night." He paused. "We are going, aren't we?"

"You bet," Leslie told him. "It's going to be great."

"Good." He reached out and gave her hand a quick squeeze. "I'd better get going. I just wanted to tell you what a good time I had last night."

"Me, too," Leslie said. Looking at Jeff now in his familiar lifeguard trunks, she found it difficult to think of him as the same guy she'd driven up to the bluffs with the night before. Last night she'd seen a different side of him.

"Well, see you later," Jeff said. He headed off down the beach, turning around once to give her a dazzling smile.

On Friday afternoon, Jeff showed up right after her lunch break, but again the beach was busy, so he couldn't stay long.

It's nice of him to make the effort to stop by even for a few minutes, Leslie thought. She adjusted her sunglasses on her nose and removed the canvas shade from the top of her lifeguard stand. This afternoon she was in the mood to work on her tan while she kept an eye on the beach.

By the time she was ready to get dressed for her date Saturday night, Leslie's skin was a lovely bronze color. She decided to wear a sleeveless white sweater and a pair of white knee-length shorts to show off her tan to its best advantage. She wondered briefly if she might have chosen the wrong outfit to wear, but decided it was better to be comfortable and casual than overdressed.

The plan was for the four of them to go to the Fun Zone in Jeff's car since it was the biggest, the flashiest, and the most fun. He was supposed to pick up Leslie, Tracy, and Fury at six-thirty, and as usual he was right on time. The doorbell rang. Leslie glanced at the time. She was relieved to see Jeff as casually dressed as she was, in a blue polo shirt (she loved him in blue) and a pair of Bermuda shorts.

They all piled into his convertible, Tracy and Fury in the backseat, and Leslie in the front next to Jeff. They sped down Surfrider into town, then turned onto the Pacific Coast Highway. The Fun Zone was right on the water, another thirty miles down the coast.

"What should we do first?" Tracy asked as they entered the amusement park.

"Let's eat," Leslie said.

"Let's go to the penny arcade," Fury said.

"Let's go on the bumper cars," Jeff said.

"Wait a second, since no one can agree, I have a better idea. Let's buy unlimited-ride wristbands. Then we can go on all the rides," Fury said.

"Good thinking," Leslie agreed.

They hurried to the ticket booth. As they waited in line, Jeff reached down to take Leslie's hand. She caught his eye and smiled.

After everyone had gotten a wristband, Tracy said, "Let's go on the Big Wave."

"The only big waves I like are the kind you can surf on," Fury admitted.

"C'mon, Fury, don't be a drag," Tracy said.

"Okay, but when I get sick, don't say I didn't warn you," he told Tracy.

They headed down the boardwalk, past the Logger's Revenge, the Pirate Ship, the bumper cars and the food stands, toward the Fun Zone's most famous ride. As they got on line for it, they could hear people shrieking and the roar of the roller coaster as it dipped and climbed and dipped again until it gradually slowed down and came to a stop. The passengers streamed out of the cars, some still screaming and laughing, and others looking green in the face.

"Are you sure you want to do this?" Jeff asked Leslie as they stepped inside the first car.

"I'm sure. I'm sure." She was more than ready to have some fun. "Are you?" she kidded him.

"I'm up for anything as long as I do it with you," he said as he scooted close to her and fastened the seat belt around them.

Tracy and Fury climbed into the car behind them.

"If you feel you're going to be sick, just do it over the side and not on me," Jeff turned around and advised Fury.

"I'll try to remember," Fury answered as the cars lurched forward.

The next thing Leslie knew, the row of cars was inching its way up to the crest of the first big wave. Everyone raised their arms and started to cheer in anticipation of the first big dip. But their warm-up shouts were mere whispers in comparison to the shrieks they let out when the cars plunged downward, taking their riders' stomachs with them. Up and down again went the cars. Jeff put his arm around Leslie, but she could tell by the way he was squeezing her that he wasn't just being affectionate. As they roared down one last

hair-raising wave, she understood why Jeff
wanted to have someone to hold onto.

"I'm going to be sick," Fury announced.

"Not on my black leather pants, you're not,"
Tracy screeched.

Leslie and Jeff just held onto each other,
screaming until the ride ended.

"Let's go on it again," Fury said.

"Oh, no. You won't get me on that again. I'm
hungry. Let's get something to eat," Jeff suggested.

"I second the idea," Tracy said.

"And I third it. You're outvoted, Fury," Leslie
said, and headed in the direction of the food
stands.

"What next?" Jeff asked when they had all
filled up on various kinds of junk food.

Leslie noticed that they were right next to
the bumper car ride. "Bumper cars," she
yelled out.

After the bumper cars, they went on the
Pirate's Ship, then the House of Mirrors and
the Scrambler.

Leslie couldn't recall when she'd last had so
much fun. It was great to have a boyfriend to
share things with. Everything seemed much
more special with Jeff around. *Who would
have guessed at the beginning of the summer*

that things would work out so well? she thought happily.

"Who's up for the Cave Train?" Jeff asked after they had staggered off the Peppermint Twist.

Leslie figured that they'd eventually get around to the Cave Train. If Jeff hadn't, she might have suggested it herself. And she knew it was just the kind of ride that Fury and Tracy would love. A few minutes later the four of them were inside a pitch-black cave. Leslie and Jeff had gotten the first car again, with the other two several feet behind. Leslie didn't even pretend to be scared by the ferocious dinosaurs that jumped out at them. She much preferred to concentrate on Jeff and his kisses. When the ride was over, this time it was Leslie who suggested going on again. Of all the rides, she liked the Cave Train by far the best.

"It's my turn to choose what to do," Fury insisted. "Let's go play some arcade games."

"You go ahead then. Leslie and I want to go on the Cave Train again," Jeff said. "We'll meet you in the penny arcade after our ride."

"Okay," Fury agreed, and he and Tracy headed for the arcade while Leslie and Jeff boarded the Cave Train again.

"I like what's happening to us," Jeff said to

Leslie as they entered the dark tunnel again. He drew her close to him and kissed her more passionately than before.

"I like what's happening to me now," Leslie told Jeff between kisses. But this time she was glad when the ride was over. Although she felt all warm and tingly inside, she didn't want to lose control.

They strolled down the boardwalk and joined Tracy and Fury in the penny arcade, where Fury was on a roll at the Pokereno game.

"How about a game of Skee Ball while we're waiting?" Jeff asked Leslie.

"Sure," she said, leaning over to put a quarter in the slot.

They ended up having a competition to see who could bowl the highest score. One hour and several dollars later, Leslie managed a score of 280 when her last ball just tipped into the fifty-point hole.

"You win," Jeff said. "I give up. You've got a pretty good arm for a girl, you know?"

Leslie glared at him, ready to blow up, but then she saw the teasing grin on his face. "I've got a better arm than a lot of guys, too," she said pointedly.

Jeff grimaced. "Ouch. Why don't I take all

those tokens and trade them in for a nice prize? Be right back," he said, and hurried off.

When he came back, he was carrying a stuffed koala bear, which he gave to Leslie. "For you, mademoiselle—a remembrance of an evening together," he said.

Leslie reached up to give Jeff a quick kiss. "Thanks, Jeff. He's adorable."

"Okay, okay, enough of this mushy stuff," Fury said as he approached them. "The Pokereno game just cleaned me out."

"You should have stopped when you were ahead like I told you," Tracy said, coming up behind him.

Fury shrugged. "You win some, you lose some. Are you two ready to go?" he asked Leslie and Jeff.

Jeff turned to Leslie. "Had enough?"

"Of the Fun Zone or you?" Leslie said flirtatiously.

"Of the Fun Zone. I know you can't get enough of me," Jeff teased back, putting his arm around her waist and heading toward the car.

Chapter 12

On Sunday morning Leslie and Tracy slept in until ten-thirty. When they got up, Leslie found that Russ and Jed had already gone out. Fury, as she could have guessed, was still sleeping. It was such a warm, sunny morning, she and Tracy decided to have Sunday brunch in their bathrobes, slippers, and sunglasses out on the deck.

"So, did you have a good time last night?" Tracy asked over her eggs Benedict.

Leslie gave her roommate a peculiar look. "'Course I did. But you know that already—you were there, remember?"

"But I wasn't with you the whole time," Tracy reminded her. "I seem to remember you and Jeff going off on your own for another ride on the Cave Train?"

Leslie blushed. "Oh, yeah."

"Don't tell me you forgot already," Tracy teased. "So, what happened?"

"We had a good time," Leslie replied, squirming under Tracy's inquistive gaze.

"That's all?" Tracy persisted.

"Okay, we had a great time!" Leslie admitted. "Oh, Tracy, I've never felt this way about a guy before. Just thinking about him makes me feel terrific. And when I'm with him I feel all breathless and tingly. Is that how you feel with Fury?"

Tracy paused before answering. "Sometimes, I guess, but not so much anymore. Our first few weeks were all sparks and fireworks, but now we seem to have more of a comfortable relationship."

"But don't you miss the sparks and fireworks?" Leslie asked.

"Well, yes and no," Tracy replied thoughtfully. "All that stuff was fun, but we were just getting to know each other. Now we know each other pretty well, and that can be just as good."

"I see what you mean," Leslie said, a

mischievous smile playing on her lips. "If Fury knows you and he likes you anyway, then you've got it made!"

"Well, what have we here?" Tracy retorted, exaggerating her slight drawl. "Leslie honey, if you're tryin' to be a comedienne, you'll have to do better than that." She leaned over and tipped Leslie's lounge chair backward so that Leslie's feet stuck up in the air. In her bathrobe and slippers, Leslie knew she must look ridiculous. "Now that's funny," Tracy said, laughing.

Monday was another perfect Southern California day. Leslie spent a slow morning on the lookout for weak swimmers and for Jeff, but only Fury showed up to relieve her at noon for lunch. When she came back after grabbing a sandwich at The Deli, Leslie lathered herself with more coconut suntan oil and settled in for a tedious afternoon. She knew she would have to be especially on guard, for the beach had certainly gotten crowded.

"Well, hello there," an elderly woman called up to her. "Do you remember me?"

Leslie looked down from her perch on the lifeguard stand. At first she had a little trouble recognizing Mrs. Owen under her wide-brimmed sun hat, but when she showed off the oversized Beachasauras T-shirt she was wearing, Leslie remembered her all too well.

"Of course I do. We met in T-Shirts For Two. You bought the shirt there. I love it on you," she called back.

"It is darling, isn't it? And it makes a wonderful coverall. I have my bathing suit underneath. I'm planning to go for a swim. See you later," Mrs. Owen said as she headed back to her beach towel and belongings just a few feet away from the tower.

Leslie watched her as she got ready to go into the water. First she took off her hat and placed it down next to her purple running shoes. Next, she slipped off her shirt to reveal an old-fashioned one-piece bathing suit with a skirt. Last but not least, she tucked her blue-gray perm inside her pink bathing cap, then made her way to the water and gingerly stepped into it. As she waded deeper into the water, Leslie was thankful for the bright cap. With lots of little kids riding body boards, inflatable animals and rings close to shore, and the older ones on surfboards farther out, it made it that much easier for Leslie to keep track of her. She had a feeling that Mrs. Owen wasn't a very strong swimmer, and she didn't want anything to happen to her.

"Hi. How's it going this afternoon?" Leslie's

heart raced. She recognized his sexy voice even before she saw his tanned, gorgeous face.

"Pretty busy," she told Jeff. He turned around and looked out toward the water to see for himself.

"I see what you mean. Sorry I couldn't get over sooner. It's like that all up and down the beach. And to make matters worse, one of the lifeguards went home sick. I had to fill in for him until Fury could relieve me," Jeff explained.

"That's okay. I understand," Leslie said.

Jeff smiled. "Are you free tonight, by any chance?"

"Sure am," Leslie replied as casually as she could. Another date with Jeff! She couldn't wait.

"Good. It's open mike at the Surfrider tonight. Want to check out the new acts? Sometimes they're pretty . . ."

While Jeff was talking, Leslie looked out to see if she could still spot the pink cap. Sure enough she could, but she didn't like what she saw. The tell-tale cap was a little too far out for Leslie's liking, and it seemed to be bobbing up and down, first in sight, then out of it. Next, she spotted the little old lady's arms flailing about in the water. No doubt about it, she was in trouble.

There was no time to explain to Jeff. Leslie threw off her visor, flew down from the platform, and sprinted across the sand toward the water. Just as she had practiced over and over in training, she dove into the water and swam with all her might toward the victim. She knew every second counted. She reached Mrs. Owen with no time to spare. She was about to go down again, and this time she might not come up. Leslie held her breath and dove under the limp body. Quickly and carefully, she flipped Mrs. Owen onto her back, and was about to bring her in when Jeff appeared out of nowhere. He pushed Leslie aside and took over, flinging his arms across Mrs. Owen's chest and under her armpit. Then he hoisted her up to rest on his hip as he towed her in to shore using the sidestroke and scissor kick.

Leslie swam after them in a state of shock. She knew Mrs. Owen would be fine in Jeff's care, but she didn't understand why he hadn't let her carry out the rescue on her own. *I didn't need his help*, she thought angrily as she waded through the shallow water to the beach. Mrs. Owen was stretched out on the sand, breathing almost normally.

"Get me an emergency blanket," Jeff barked at her.

Leslie bristled, but did as she was told. No matter how angry she was, Mrs. Owen's safety came first. *He has some nerve!* she thought as she retrieved the foil blanket from her stand. *I could have completed the rescue just as well as he did. What does he think I would have done if he hadn't been here?*

When she returned with the blanket, a crowd had gathered around Jeff and Mrs. Owen. To add insult to injury, Jeff was now basking in the glory he did not deserve. While Leslie wrapped the emergency blanket around Mrs. Owen and did her best to comfort her, he was fielding questions from the local newspaper reporter who covered the beach beat.

"How did you know she was in trouble?" he asked, taking out a notebook and pencil from his shirt pocket.

"I saw her thrashing in the water," Jeff answered.

He saw me *spotting her thrashing in the water,* Leslie fumed.

"How long have you been a lifeguard?"

"Four years."

That's four years too many, Leslie thought to herself.

"How many rescues have you made?"

"Oh, about forty."

Correction, Leslie muttered to herself. *Thirty-nine and one steal.*

"What's your full name?"

"Jeffrey Porter."

"Jeff, tell me, what advice can you give our readers so they can avoid getting in trouble in the water?"

"Well, first of all, if you're not a strong swimmer, I would advise not swimming in water over your head."

Leslie could tell that Jeff was eating up all the attention. But as far as she was concerned he was in water over his head with her. And this time she didn't plan to rescue him by making excuses for his actions. She knew for sure now that they spoke louder than his words and that she should have trusted her instincts. Jeff's overbearing and overprotective behavior last week had not been a unique occurrence as Leslie had hoped. No, he had simply revealed the true Jeff—and now that Leslie knew him, she didn't like him at all.

"And equally important, I advise everyone to spend a few minutes wave-watching before entering the water. Especially kids. They should enter the water as though they were crossing a busy street. Be alert and don't get caught in the shallows in big pounding surf," he went on.

"That's great stuff, Jeff. Can you repeat your advice to the kids so I can get it all down?" the reporter asked Jeff.

Leslie watched as he gladly repeated it for the reporter's benefit.

While the newspaperman wrote down his every word, Leslie became even more furious with Jeff. What had he done? Written a pre-pared speech? Or was this the spiel he always gave to make himself look good? Leslie was amazed at how much she was learning about Jeff. She thanked her lucky stars that she had found out more about him before she'd gotten herself in deeper water.

Mrs. Owen struggled to sit up. "Isn't your boyfriend's name Jeff?" she asked. "Is that him?" She sounded as if she was as impressed with Jeff as he was with himself.

Leslie was glad that her new friend was acting more like her old self, but she wasn't in the mood to hear her sing Jeff's praises.

"Not anymore," she said, anxious to get back to her station and out of earshot of Jeff's conceited interview.

"Oh, too bad," Mrs. Owen said.

When the reporter noticed that she was sitting up and talking, he came over and started asking her questions. Leslie used the opportunity to escape back to the tower. She would have loved to give Jeff a piece of her mind, but she was so angry with him, she knew if she even started talking, she'd explode.

But Jeff made the mistake of catching up with her as she headed back. "Wow, that was a close call," he said. "It was a good thing I was in the vicinity."

That was the last straw. Leslie had had more than enough of Jeff's patronizing attitude toward her and his overblown opinion of himself.

"And what was I sitting up there for—decoration?" she asked sarcastically.

"Leslie, don't get so upset. That's not what I meant."

"What do you mean?" she asked, putting her hands on her hips and glaring at him.

"I only meant that I was glad I was in the vicinity to assist you."

"Assist? Assist? You call that an assist? I call it an outright steal!"

"Leslie, calm down. You're blowing this whole thing out of proportion. I was only trying to help you. I thought you might not be able to handle the situation. What if the victim had struggled? Took you under with her? Or rolled over on you?"

"Nothing would have happened," Leslie declared confidently. "I am a qualified life-guard, remember? I was hired over hundreds of guys because I could handle that very situation better and faster than they could." She took a deep breath, then burst out in another rage. "Just because I'm a girl doesn't mean I'm helpless. I think you'd better revise your opinion of women. You're about a hundred years out of date."

Jeff was quiet for several seconds. Then he said apologetically, "Look, I'm sorry. I didn't mean to upset you. So let's change the subject. Do you want to go for dinner before we go to the Surfrider Cafe?"

Leslie wasn't about to fall for one of his phony apologies. "You really don't understand, do you?"

"Of course I do," Jeff said, but she could see that he didn't.

"Let me explain it to you," Leslie said as if she were talking to a little kid. "I don't want to go to dinner with you. I don't want to go anywhere with you. In fact, except on the job, I don't want to see you or go out with you anymore."

Jeff looked completely crushed. "C'mon,

Leslie, let's at least go out tonight and talk this over. I'm sure we can work this out." His voice had that sexy quality that had always won her over in the past. But this time she didn't let it get to her.

"I don't think so, Jeff. Now if you'll excuse me, I have to get back to work," she told him firmly, then turned to climb back into her tower.

"Well, if that's how you feel." He turned away from her, and without saying another word, darted over to the little old lady to help her gather up her belongings. Leslie felt no remorse as she watched the two of them walk off the beach.

Chapter 13

It came as a relief to Leslie that Jeff didn't show his face again the rest of the day. If there were any way she could avoid seeing him all summer, she'd be even happier. She still couldn't believe the stunt he'd pulled. But there was the whole story—"Head Lifeguard Makes Brave Rescue"—in the evening edition of the *Marina Bay Beacon*.

Leslie wanted to throw up all over Jeff's front page picture. *I don't think I've ever met a more conceited jerk*, she thought as she passed the newsstand and dashed across the street to T-Shirts For Two. She had left work on the dot of five to see Tracy before she left the store. Luckily, she caught her getting ready to close up for the night.

"Tracy, I've just got to talk to you," Leslie huffed, trying to catch her breath.

"At your service. Where should we go to talk? I was just about to leave."

"Let's go to the soda shop."

Tracy locked up the store and the two girls walked next door to the Flotsam and Jetsamwich Soda Shop. Leslie was glad that, except for a group of giggly preteen girls at the counter, the soda shop was empty. She walked to the back and slid into a red and white upholstered booth in the far corner.

"So, what's the emergency today?" Tracy asked, taking the seat opposite. "No, don't tell me. You and Jeff are eloping and you want me to come along and be a bridesmaid."

"I wouldn't marry him if he was the last man on earth," Leslie declared.

"What'll it be, girls?" the waiter asked, approaching their table with an order pad in his hand.

"A diet Coke, please," Tracy said.

"Make that two," Leslie said. "No, on second thought, I'll have a root beer float."

"My, that's a sudden change of heart," Tracy commented.

"You mean ordering a root beer float?" Leslie asked.

"About Jeff, silly. Not the soda. Would you mind filling me in on how you went from being head over heels in love with him last night to not wanting to marry him if he were the last man on earth?"

"Tracy, I can't believe I ever thought I was in love with him. I've lost all respect for him, and as of this afternoon I've broken up with him." Leslie tried to keep her anger under control as she recounted how Jeff had stolen the rescue and, even more infuriating, the glory. She had just finished her story when their drinks arrived.

Tracy took a big sip of her soda. "That was a pretty rotten, male-chauvinist thing for him to do," she said. "I can't say I blame you for breaking up with him over it." Tracy took another long sip. "But the good news is, that means you're free tonight."

"Tonight and every other night, probably for the rest of the summer."

"Don't be so negative. Remember what I told you about how to attract a guy. It worked before and it can work again. What you need right now is a change of scene. It's open mike at the Surfrider and I'm planning to sing. Why don't you come?" Tracy suggested. "That

should take your mind off Jeff. Maybe you'll
even meet someone tonight."

"That's funny, Trace," Leslie said thoughtfully. "Jeff wanted to take me to the Surfrider
tonight. But I'm sure he had no idea you were
singing. How come you didn't tell me?"

"Because I only just decided to. Tell Russ
and Jed to come, too. Open mike begins at
eight. I'll tell Fury. Which reminds me. I'm
meeting him at five-thirty for some fish and
chips on the pier. Then I have to rush back to
the house to pick up my guitar. What time is
it?"

"Five-thirty."

Tracy drained her glass in one long, last sip.
"I've got to run."

"Thanks for lending an ear. The Coke's on
me. I'll see you later," Leslie said, then started
on her soda. By now the ice cream was half
melted. She stirred what was left of the scoop
into the soda and watched it dissolve and fizz,
then gulped it down quickly. She wasn't in the
mood to sit around the soda shop by herself.
Maybe, she thought, putting down her glass,
she shouldn't have chug-a-lugged it. She
needed to practice nursing a drink and being
alone.

Don't be so melodramatic, she scolded
herself, and reached for the check. *Breaking*

up with Jeff isn't the end of the world. He's not the only guy in Marina Bay. There must be a lot of guys out there who are nicer than Jeff, she thought. *Who knows? Like Tracy said, maybe I'll meet someone at the Surfrider tonight.* Leslie decided right then and there that, with the help of Tracy's famous body-language formula, she'd start looking for Jeff's replacement that night.

As soon as Leslie got home, she passed the word around about Tracy's performance at the Surfrider. Jed offered to drive everyone into town in his van. And Russ called his buddy Chris, who in turn called Erica and Maggie. Fury and Tracy arrived home not long after Leslie, and while Tracy changed her clothes and picked up her guitar, Fury called his surfing buddies, Nick and Danny. Everyone wanted to make sure that there would be a big crowd to give Tracy some moral support.

"Wish me luck, gang," Tracy said as she headed out the door with Fury. She looked terrific in a red satin embroidered shirt and black jeans. With her dark curly hair cascading down her back, all she needed was a ten-gallon hat to make her look like a real cowgirl. Her face, however, was pale with fright.

"If you sing half as well tonight as you

usually do in the shower, you'll be great," Leslie assured her.

By the time the whole gang had gathered at the Surfrider to hear Tracy sing, they took up an entire round table. But tonight, instead of their usual table in the corner under the fern, Leslie suggested that they sit right up front. Besides being able to see and hear Tracy better, she had another reason for being so visible. If Jeff happened to show up, she wanted to be sure he saw her surviving very well without him.

News of Jeff's rescue arrived before he did. Chris had picked up the evening paper on the way in and now sat next to Leslie reading the article out loud. "Hey, Jeff's a real hero. Did you see the rescue, Leslie?"

"Did I see it? Ha! That's a joke," Leslie answered. Then she told Chris and the others what had really happened.

"That's too bad. I bet it'll be pretty hard for you to be anything but all business with him for the rest of the summer," Chris said in a sympathetic voice, scooting his chair closer to Leslie's.

"You've got that right," Leslie replied, detecting Chris's subtle way of double checking that she and Jeff were no longer an item before putting his arm on the back of her chair. She'd known Chris for ages—ever since he and Russ had played their first volleyball game years ago—but she'd never thought of him in a romantic way until now. It was a strange feeling, but not bad. It might take her a while to get used to it, but in the meantime she decided to enjoy the special attention.

Chris was about to say something more to her when Will, the emcee and owner of the Surfrider, stepped up to the microphone. Leslie paid little attention to him as he announced the opening act, for at that same moment she spotted Jeff walking into the cafe with Miss Popular, of all people, attached to his arm. With most of her long legs showing, Leslie hated to admit that she looked just as good in a miniskirt and tight sweater as she had the day she strutted past her on the beach in a skimpy bathing suit.

Well, Jeff didn't waste any time getting his new act together. So, why should I? she fumed to herself. She decided that now was the time to try Tracy's body-language technique. She leaned her head back on her chair. Chris took the hint and lowered his arm from the back of the chair to around her shoulder. His timing was perfect. Jeff couldn't avoid noticing them on his way to the only empty table for two, which happened to be right next to where Leslie's group was sitting.

As he approached, Leslie nuzzled into the crook of Chris's arm and glared at Jeff and his date. When he caught her gaze, Jeff looked away from her. But Miss Popular stared right back with an "I've got him now" look of her own.

Leslie did her best to not let it get to her, but she couldn't help it. *Why do I care that Jeff is out with snotty Miss Popular?* she thought. *They both have inflated egos the size of the Goodyear blimp—they belong together.* But still the awful sensation in the pit of her stomach persisted. "I'm not going to dwell on this another minute," Leslie said under her breath, and let herself be distracted by the stand-up comic's closing joke on stage.

Leslie broke into laughter, then applause, along with the entire audience. She was sorry now that she had missed the rest of the comic's routine.

"Good night, folks. You've been a great audience," he shouted over the applause and rushed off stage.

When Will welcomed Tracy Berberian, "a rising new star from the heart of Fresno," and the spotlight highlighted her shiny red satin Western shirt, Leslie made up her mind to give her friend her undivided attention and Jeff and his date not another minute's thought. That was easy to do. Leslie was so captivated by Tracy's shimmering presence on stage that she was even unconscious of Chris's arm still around her.

At first, Leslie could tell that Tracy was nervous. Her brows were knit together in concentration. But as she progressed through her set, she obviously gained confidence, even smiling slightly as she belted out the words to several Country Western favorites. Although Leslie didn't normally consider herself a Country Western fan, with Tracy as a roommate she'd learned to like it. Besides, Tracy's voice was so smooth and clear, Leslie was convinced she could make anything sound good.

Her last song, though, was extra special. Called "Heart Over Mind," she had written it herself. She seemed to be singing the song to Fury, who sat in his seat with an embarrassed grin on his face. But the last few lines reminded Leslie of Jeff.

"Heart over mind, sometimes you've got to give in

Change a little, make a compromise
Heart over mind if you're gonna let love win."

Tracy drew out the last note and ended her
act by taking a sweeping bow. "Let's give
talented Tracy a big hand," Will said, stepping
up to the mike. But he really didn't have to
encourage this audience. Leslie, Chris, Fury,
Russ, Jed, everyone at the table, were already
on their feet applauding. Others in the cafe,
even Jeff and Miss Popular, followed their lead
and stood up to applaud and whistle their
approval. "Encore, encore," several people
shouted.

"We'll have Tracy come back for Nashville
Night," Will promised. "But tonight we still
have lots more entertainment for you. So
settle down and let's get on with it."

Leslie sat back down, bursting with pride
over her roommate's success. *Tracy's sure to
be a big star some day*, she thought, leaning
back in her chair. As she did, she realized that
Chris had put his arm around her again. Leslie
tried to relax, but after Tracy's rousing number she found it hard to concentrate on the
mediocre juggling act now on stage. Chris,
too, Leslie noticed, was fidgety and looked
like he wanted to be somewhere else.

"I'm starving. Let's go get something to eat," he suggested. "We won't be able to get anything here until the show is over."

Leslie was in her glory as she and Chris said their farewells in between acts and cut out. As they walked out of the Surfrider and down to the pier for some food, Chris still had his arm stiffly around her shoulder as if it had been glued there. Although it still seemed unnatural to be with Chris, she hoped that Jeff and his new girl friend had seen them leave the cafe together.

"My truck's parked close by on Windward Way. I know a nice spot up on the bluffs. Why don't we drive on up and eat there?" Chris suggested, handing Leslie her fish and chips from the Hungry Pelican take-out stand.

The last thing she could picture herself doing was parking up on the bluffs in Chris's funky old flatbed truck. *With my luck he'll probably want to take me to the same place Jeff did,* Leslie thought. *What do these guys do? Rotate the spot?* she joked to herself. But when she recalled her romantic evening with Jeff on the bluffs, she didn't feel like laughing.

"I thought you were really hungry," Leslie said. "It's really nice by the water. Why don't we just eat here?" The half moon made the ocean shimmer and it was bright enough so that they could eat their take-out by moonlight alone.

Chris shrugged. "Sure. Good idea," he said, and led her over to a bench along the pier.

"So, how's your summer been going?" Chris asked, making small talk between big bites of his fish fillet.

"Great, up until today." Leslie munched on a fry.

"Oh, sorry, Leslie. That was a dumb question."

"That's okay. I'm getting over it. How's yours going?"

"Lousy, up until tonight."

Leslie knew exactly what Chris was implying, but pretended she didn't. "How come? I thought you and Russ were playing a lot of volleyball."

"Too much. I could use a vacation from my vacation. I'm almost thinking of looking for a job."

"Oh, don't do that. What would Russ do all day?" Leslie teased.

"You're right," Chris said with a grin. "If I got a job, what would happen to Marina Bay's dynamic duo?" He paused and looked at Leslie pointedly. "Maybe all I need is a little diversion."

Now Leslie was really on the spot. *Chris is certainly one of the nicer guys in Marina Bay*, she told herself, but somehow even that thought didn't make her more enthusiastic. *Well*, Leslie thought, *from the moment Chris sat down next to me in the cafe, I haven't exactly objected. In all honesty, I've been encouraging him. But after all*, she decided, *isn't a little diversion exactly what I've been looking for?*

Chapter 14

"Hi, what's happening?" Chris called up to her.

"Not much. Same old stuff."

It was four o'clock on Friday and Leslie was still on duty. Ordinarily, she'd be on her break around this time, but Fury had called in sick and Jeff had obviously made a point of not coming himself to relieve her.

The only communication she'd had with him since their breakup was a memo from him delivered by Fury on Wednesday reminding her to keep next Saturday night free for the annual lifeguard ocean competition. According to Jeff's note, Leslie was slotted to be one

of four swimmers in the relay race. Jeff had
told her ages ago about his plan to send a
team to represent Marina Bay Beach at the
competition traditionally held at Torrance
Beach forty miles down the coast. But after
not seeing him all week, she hadn't been sure
whether he still planned on including her.
She'd thought perhaps he'd decided that as a
girl, she might hold back the team. At least
now she knew he wasn't that much of a
chauvinist.

If Jeff had gotten out of the habit of dropping by her lifeguard stand, Chris had gotten
into it. He took regular breaks from his
volleyball to come and see her, often bringing
her a cup of coffee and something to munch
on.

"I brought you something," he said now,
reaching up to hand her a paper sack.

"Thanks, Chris, I'm fading fast," she said,
taking a container of coffee and a jelly dough-
nut from the bag.

He shrugged. "No problem."

"Seriously, you're a lifesaver," Leslie said.
She did appreciate his visits and all the snacks
he brought with him—they helped to ease the
boredom—but she also felt guilty. Guilty because she didn't return Chris's feelings.

"Um, Leslie," Chris began hesitantly, "I

know a great swimming beach just up the coast. How about we hit it tomorrow?"

Leslie's guilt instantly grew more intense. From all the attention he had been showering on her since Monday night, Leslie had suspected that volleyball had become his little diversion and she was now his main interest. But up until now, he hadn't actually asked her on a date. Something inside her told her she kind of liked it that way.

Leslie took a sip of coffee and thought a moment. "I'm sorry, Chris, but I've got plans for tomorrow," she said. "Jed has the day off and I promised I'd go windsurfing with him." Jed wasn't just a convenient excuse. He had been pestering her all week to go with him, and in truth, she felt she owed him one.

"Oh," Chris looked really disappointed. "What about tomorrow night?"

"Tomorrow night?" Leslie paused before answering. "I think I'm free tomorrow night." Although she thought Chris was an awfully sweet guy, she could sense by the way she hesitated before agreeing to go out with him that something was wrong. For starters, there wasn't even the slightest hint of sparks and fireworks. But Leslie felt that she owed him one date, at least, to figure out how she really felt about him.

"Great. Let's get out of Marina Bay. Maybe hit the mall at Valley Vista."

"That sounds like fun. I haven't been to the mall in ages," Leslie said, trying to work up some interest in Chris's plan. But she knew that even if he had suggested driving into Los Angeles to take in a baseball game or to go window shopping on Rodeo Drive, she wouldn't have been all that excited. *It's been a long week. You're just tired. After a night off, you'll feel differently*, she told herself, trying to give Chris the benefit of the doubt.

"I'll pick you up around seven. Why don't we plan on eating dinner out there?"

"Sure." Leslie hoped the tone of her voice didn't betray her lack of enthusiasm for the idea. She envisioned them chowing down on egg rolls, pizza, or nachos at the International Cafe, a glorified cafeteria in the center of the mall that specialized in fast foods from around the world. It certainly lacked the class of Port of Call on the pier, where Jeff had taken her. But there was no point now in making any comparisons. Her relationship with Jeff was over and she had no regrets, she had to remind herself.

"So, I'll see you tomorrow night then," Chris said. "Bye."

Leslie watched Chris head back in the

direction of the volleyball courts, then glanced down at her Swatch. In just thirty minutes she'd be off for the weekend. She amused herself for the next half hour by observing several brown pelicans, one behind the other, gracefully skim over the water, then suddenly break formation and dive-bomb for anchovies. The next time she looked at her Swatch it was five o'clock. "T.G.I.F.," she mumbled to herself as she slipped on her sneakers, gathered up her gear, and climbed down from the tower. She raced across the sand to the car, then sped straight home, anxious to take a nap before thinking about dinner.

"Anybody home?" Leslie called out as she walked through the door.

"I am," Jed said, coming in from the deck. Water dripped from his sandy-colored hair and wet suit. "Are we still on for windsurfing tomorrow?" he asked.

"Sure, we're still on for windsurfing tomorrow. So why are you wearing your wet suit now? Planning on getting a real early start?" Leslie couldn't help staring at Jed in his wet suit. It bulged out everywhere, but especially in the stomach, thighs, and rear, and Leslie couldn't decide if he looked more like a pregnant seal or the Michelin tire man.

"I was just trying it on to see how it fit in the water," Jed explained.

"I can't say I blame you. Knowing how you windsurf, you'll be spending most of your time there," Leslie kidded Jed. "Where is everyone else?" she wondered aloud.

"Russ is playing volleyball . . ."

With Chris, no doubt, Leslie thought.

"And Fury and Tracy are in town," Jed told her.

"It's a miracle how a day off can cure whatever ails you," Leslie commented, recalling that Fury had called in sick to work that morning.

"You can say that again. I can't wait until mine tomorrow," Jed said, all excited.

"I can. What time do you want to get started?"

"How about eight o'clock? The early bird catches the worm."

"C'mon, Jed. Give me a break. We're not going fishing, you know."

"Okay. How does ten sound?"

"A little more civilized. I'm really pooped. I'm going to lie down," Leslie said, climbing the stairs wearily. She had a feeling she'd need as much energy as she could muster for Jed's windsurfing lesson the following day.

Chapter 15

The next sound Leslie heard was Jed pounding on her bedroom door and shouting, "C'mon, Leslie, get up. It's almost ten o'clock."

She looked down at her Swatch. Jed was right. It was a quarter to ten. What had she done? Slept through the night? Outside her bedroom window was yet another sunny Southern California day. Apparently she had. She still had her watch on and the aqua and pink Arena she had worn yesterday. She knew she had felt bone tired when she'd kicked off her shorts and sneakers and flopped onto her bed for a little snooze. But she hadn't expected to sleep through the night and, if Jed hadn't awakened her, probably the morning as well. Her emotionally draining week had finally caught up with her, she realized.

Jed pounded on the door again. "Leslie, are you in there? If you don't answer, I'm coming in," he threatened.

"I'm up. I'm up. I'll be down in a minute," Leslie shouted back, hopping out of bed. Quickly she washed up and changed into a clean tank suit, then grabbed a towel from the bathroom, her visor and Vuarnets from her beach bag, and flew downstairs.

"See? I'm up and raring to go," Leslie boasted as she walked into the kitchen to pour herself a cup of coffee.

"After that marathon sleep, you should feel quite refreshed. Want a piece of toast? I've already buttered some."

"Jed, you're a doll," Leslie said as he passed over the bread basket. Leslie wolfed down two slices of toast, then washed them down with two cups of coffee before saying to Jed, "Now, let's get this show on the road."

"I've already brought the boom, sail, and board down to the water's edge," Jed informed her as they stepped off the deck and onto the warm sand. The morning sun was already quite bright. Leslie slipped on her sunglasses and visor.

"Good start," she said as they headed toward Jed's equipment.

"Do you know how to rig your sail?" Leslie asked when they reached the water.

"Not really."

"Okay. I'll show you, then next time you can do it yourself."

Expertly, Leslie rigged the sail, then she and Jed floated the board out just beyond the waves to where they could still stand. Under Leslie's direction, Jed put the centerboard in place.

"That was the easy part. Now comes the tricky part. Are you ready to try to stand up?"

"I was born ready," Jed said with obvious false confidence.

"Okay. First kneel on the board." Jed got into a kneeling position. "When I'm done explaining this next part, stand up and try to get your balance. Don't be afraid of the board tipping. With the centerboard in, it won't tip that easily," Leslie informed him. "Now, when you think you have your balance, reach down and grab the rope connected to the boom.

When you pull the boom up and toward you, the sail will also come up. Then lean back and hold the sail from the wind. Have you got all that?"

"I think so." Jed had gotten it, all right. The next thing Leslie knew, he and the sail were up. The wind was just gusty enough to get a beginner going. The sail billowed, and Jed moved quickly out to sea under its power. But before Leslie even had a chance to worry that Jed was going out too far, she saw him fall off the board into the water, and swam out to him.

"That was terrific," Leslie shouted while treading water. "Now get back on the board and start all over again." When Jed was back on, Leslie said, "I forgot to tell you one important thing. You can turn the board by shifting the sail. If you bring the sail toward you, you turn right, away from you, you turn left. Got that?"

"I got it."

On this try and many more that followed, Jed proved to Leslie that his first time up and sailing was beginner's luck. He would no sooner be standing on the board when, splash—the boom, sail, and Jed were all back in the water. Finally, after about the thirtieth try, he got the knack a little and got up and moving again. But there were only so many dousings Jed could take.

"I think I've had enough for one day," he admitted to Leslie.

Leslie instructed him to pull up the centerboard, lower the sail, and let the board run aground on shore. When Jed, his equipment, and instructor were all beached again, Leslie wrapped her towel around her shoulders. "You should be proud of yourself. Not everybody gets up and sailing on the first day."

Jed broke into a big grin and said, "I owe it all to a great teacher. Thanks, Leslie. It was really nice of you to give me a lesson on your day off. I hope I didn't stop you from doing anything special."

"Don't think twice about it. I only gave up going for a drive up the coast to this great beach with Chris," she said.

She'd meant it as a joke, but as soon as she saw the expression on Jed's face change, she wished she could take back her words. He no longer looked happy and proud of himself, but shamefully guilty.

"There I go again. Why is it I always say the wrong thing when I'm with you? I'm sorry, Jed. To tell you the truth, I was glad to have an excuse not to go with Chris today."

"Oh sure," Jed replied sarcastically.

"No, I'm serious," Leslie insisted. "Besides, I have a date with him tonight instead."

"That's nice," Jed said, and began gathering his windsurfing equipment.

Leslie watched him quietly. *I can't believe it,* she thought. *Only last week I was complaining that I didn't have any guys interested in me. Now all of a sudden there's Jed, who I thought was only teasing about his crush on me, but now it seems that he's serious. And then there's Chris, who is another surprise. And then there's Jeff . . .*

"Here, let me give you a hand with that stuff," she said to Jed, quickly getting up to help.

Leslie picked up the boom and sail and carried them toward the house while Jed handled the board. When they reached the deck, Leslie turned to Jed and said, "You know, I really did have a good time today. You were a great student. If you ever want another lesson, just ask."

"Thanks, Les," Jed replied flatly.

"Jed, I mean it," she said. "Look, you've become one of my best buddies this summer. I'm flattered that you want me to teach you how to windsurf." Leslie cringed when she said the "best buddies" part, for she remembered how she used to hate it when guys said something like that to her. But she couldn't think of any other way to put it.

"I'm glad you're flattered," Jed said, smiling again as they entered the house. "It looks like I'm going to need many more lessons!"

Chapter 16

After thirty minutes at the mall that evening with Chris, Leslie remembered why she hadn't been there in ages. Kids three or four years younger than herself milled around their favorite stores in large groups, eating, talking, screaming. And at the International Cafe, the noise and congestion were compounded by messy tables and food fights. One taste of the egg rolls from the Golden Pagoda Pavilion and Leslie understood perfectly why the preteen set preferred to fire them at each other like hand grenades rather than eat them. It was hard for her to believe that only a few years ago she had thought that eating at the International Cafe was the closest thing to heaven.

After dinner, they browsed through the stores, pretending to be interested in the summer sales. Although Chris held her hand nearly the whole evening, they didn't talk much, and Leslie felt very uncomfortable. She had to admit to herself that Chris was not the guy for her, no matter how hard she tried. That special feeling just wasn't there.

"Want to go for some dessert?" Chris asked when they were back in his truck again.

"I'm not feeling too well," Leslie said. "I think it was something I ate." Actually, she wasn't just trying to beg off. The egg rolls from dinner still sat in her stomach like petrified rocks. But what also weighted her down was the thought that she'd have to level with him before the evening was over.

Leslie waited until almost the last possible moment before working up the courage to say something. "How's your volleyball going?" she asked innocently enough as Chris pulled up in front of her house.

"Great. It's really good to play with Russ. If I say so myself, we make one heck of a team."

"That's great." She took a deep breath. Now

came the hard part. "Look, Chris, I like you a lot," she said at last. "But I've got to be honest with you. I don't think you and I make such a great team." She could hardly believe that she was now telling Russ's best friend that she didn't want to see him. Hadn't it been just less than a week ago when she had broken up with her own boss? If she kept this up, she'd break all kinds of records for breaking up.

"I guess you're right," Chris agreed, to Leslie's surprise. He hadn't even hesitated. "You're a great girl, Leslie. And I have to admit, I've been wanting to go out with you for a while now, but you're right. I don't think we're meant for each other."

Leslie reached over and gave his hand a quick squeeze. "Thanks for tonight. You don't have to walk me to the door. I can see myself in," Leslie said, breathing a lot easier. Her little talk with Chris had gone better than she had expected.

"Say, could you tell Russ to meet me at the volleyball court tomorrow at ten," Chris said as Leslie climbed down from the truck. Leslie thought he sounded relieved, too.

"Sure," she said as she headed up the walk-way.

The house was quiet when Leslie got inside,

but she could see the light on beneath Russ's closed door. Darn. She'd had a feeling that Russ might wait up to ask her if she'd had a good time with Chris. He'd be very disappointed to find out what had happened, but she really wasn't in the mood to tell him. All she really wanted to do now was close her eyes and wake up to a new day.

She crept up the stairs and down the hall. "Russ, Chris says to meet him at the volleyball courts at ten tomorrow," she called out as she passed his door. Then she hurried down the hall to her own room before he could stop her.

Once she entered the sanctuary of her room, Leslie shut the door behind her and heaved a weary sigh. But as she let out her breath, she felt all her pent-up emotions coming to the surface. She made it to her bed just in time to bury her head in the pillow before bursting into tears.

"What's the matter, Les?" Tracy asked in concern. She put down the magazine she'd been reading and came over to sit on the bed beside Leslie.

"I don't know," she mumbled.

"Why don't you sit up and wipe your eyes?" Tracy said softly. Leslie sat up and took the tissues her roommate handed her. She dabbed her eyes until she felt more in control.

"Can you talk now?"

Leslie nodded her head.

"Now tell me. What's wrong?"

"Oh, Tracy, everything. I've blown everything. My date with Chris tonight was a disaster. Chris is a nice guy, but I don't know . . ."

"So you and Chris didn't hit it off. Big deal. You've only gone out with him once. I wouldn't cry my eyes out over it."

"It's not just Chris. Jed, too. I don't want to hurt him, but I just don't feel the same way about him that he feels about me. He makes me feel so guilty sometimes."

"But the one person you're really crying about you still haven't mentioned."

"Who's that?" Leslie asked. She already knew the answer only too well, but she didn't want to admit it.

"Jeff Porter. Remember him," Tracy said.

"Jeff? That's a laugh. You think I'm crying over Jeff?"

"Yes. I think you're crying over Jeff."

Leslie gave a wry smile through her tears. "I guess it's kind of obvious. If I'm crying over Jeff, does it mean that I'm not over him?" she asked.

"No, it means you're not over crying over him. Think about it, Leslie. You never did give yourself time to get over him. You went from Jeff's arms right into Chris's."

"My story sounds like one of your songs," she remarked. "The next line should be 'You traded Jeff's hugs for Chris's kisses.' Except I didn't. It just wasn't right with Chris. Oh, Tracy. I wanted it to work out with Chris, Jeff, anybody. Thanks to you, I've gotten great at attracting guys. But I need to sign up for the second part of your course—how to keep them around."

"Say, you're not the only one with that problem. I don't know if it means anything, but Fury's been pretty restless lately."

Leslie looked at her roommate in surprise. "What do you mean? You two are perfect for each other."

"I know that, but to Fury his freedom is the most important thing." Tracy shrugged. "It's probably just a phase. I'm sure we'll be okay."

"Guys sure are weird, aren't they?" Leslie remarked. "I don't know why I'm so particular. The summer's almost half over and I still don't have anything romantic going."

"The summer's not over yet, and neither are your chances for a summer romance," Tracy declared. "Things will work out. You'll see."

"I just don't know how you can be so sure," Leslie said.

"Have I given you bad advice so far?"

Leslie shook her head.

"Then trust me."

Leslie was still skeptical, but she felt better anyway. So, she didn't have a boyfriend. Big deal! She had someone equally as valuable, someone who was always willing to listen and give advice, someone she could count on.

She reached out and gave her roommate an affectionate hug. "I've never known anyone like you. Thanks, Tracy, for being such a good friend."

Chapter 17

Now that Leslie had her head on straight again, starting on Monday she decided to devote all her free time to preparing for the annual lifeguard ocean competition. It was just as well, she thought, that there weren't any men in her life right now to distract her. She had arranged with Tracy and Fury to meet her at the beach just beyond her lifeguard station right after work. Fury was scheduled to do the rescue-board paddle leg of the relay race, and Tracy had agreed to help them both practice. Leslie was determined that Marina

Bay would win the race, but most of all, she wanted to prove that she was just as capable as any of the guys.

It was a quarter past five on Monday evening and Leslie, Tracy, and Fury with his rescue board were at the water's edge getting ready for their first practice session. Leslie dipped her big toe in the ocean. The water was still quite pleasant, she thought, considering the time of day. At eight o'clock on Saturday night, when she would be swimming the race for real, she knew the water wouldn't be as warm.

"Okay, here's how you can help us," Leslie said to Tracy, handing her a stopwatch. "Fury and I will simulate our leg of the relay race. Fury will paddle out one hundred meters on the rescue board, then turn around and come back to shore. When he touches me, I'll swim out and back the same distance. Your job is to record our individual and combined times."

For the next five nights in a row Tracy clocked their times until Leslie felt they couldn't improve on them. At first, Fury was reluctant to give up all his evenings, but by Wednesday night he had caught Leslie's fever and was working hard to improve his time.

On Friday evening after their final workout,

Leslie asked a very fatigued Fury, "So what do you think? Are you satisfied with your time?"

"I don't think I could make that board go any faster unless I had bionic arms."

"I thought you had. Make a muscle and let's see," Tracy said. Wearing just his wet cut-offs, Fury flexed his arms and struck a pose like a he-man. To everyone's surprise—but mostly his own—his biceps bulged.

"No bully on the beach will mistake me for a ninety-pound weakling anymore."

"My hero," Tracy said to Fury. "Now let's see yours," she said to Leslie.

"This is dumb," Leslie said, flexing her muscle, but sure enough, her muscle appeared and it certainly was solid.

"Wowee! Look at that," Tracy said. "You must eat lots of spinach or something, like Popeye."

"Man, you're in great shape," Fury commented.

"Okay, enough show and tell. Don't forget, Fury and I are still in training. I suggest we tank up on complex carbohydrates tonight, then get a good night's rest. I'll make spaghetti for dinner."

Leslie was quite serious. She knew that the men would heavily outnumber the women in tomorrow night's competition and she wanted to do well, not only for herself but to show that women were equal to men as lifeguards. Jeff would certainly have to change his attitude then—and boy, would she make him pay.

When they returned home, Leslie quickly changed out of her wet suit and, as she had promised, headed into the kitchen to make the spaghetti dinner.

Jed put down his book on windsurfing and came in from the deck to help. "What can I do?" he asked.

"Why don't you make some garlic bread?"

Fury and Tracy soon joined the two cooks. While Leslie put up the spaghetti and warmed up the bottled sauce, Tracy made a salad and Fury set the table.

Just when everything was ready and Leslie was about to serve dinner, Russ came in from playing volleyball, all sandy and sweaty and, of course, hungry. "Hmm, something smells good," he said. "I don't suppose I'm invited for dinner."

"Russ, in addition to all your other talents, I didn't know you were a mind reader," Leslie remarked. "Sit down. It's almost ready."

Russ didn't need another invitation to join

them at the dining room table. "So, tomorrow's the big meet. Are you excited, Fury?"

"Yeah. Are you planning to come?" Fury asked Russ.

"I wouldn't miss it for the world."

Jed looked up from buttering the Italian bread. "I'm driving down in the van tomorrow afternoon. Does anyone want a ride?"

"Sure. It would be fun if we all rode down together," Tracy answered.

Leslie had been planning to drive down in the Suzuki, but if everyone else was going to go in the van, she didn't want to miss out. Besides, she'd need her friends to give her a pep talk on the way down.

"Jeff tells me you and Fury have been practicing for the meet all week," Russ commented to Leslie. "Do you feel ready for the big race?"

"How does Jeff know we've been practicing?" Leslie replied in surprise.

Russ shrugged. "How should I know. Maybe he has his spies out."

"On Tuesday morning he asked me if I wanted to work out with him and I told him that you and I were already in training," Fury admitted.

"What did he say when you told him?" Leslie was curious to know.

"He seemed very impressed. He said with that kind of enthusiasm, we should have a good chance of winning."

Leslie was surprised to hear that Jeff had anything nice to say about her. *Maybe he's already thinking twice about his sexist attitude*, she thought. *After I beat out all the guys in tomorrow's race, he'll definitely have to change his attitude.* She set the bowl of spaghetti on the table with a determined smile.

"Dig in, everyone," she said, but everyone already had.

Chapter 18

"I forgot a towel. Could you grab one for me, Russ?" Leslie yelled up to him as she was rushing out the door Saturday afternoon. Russ raced out of the house a few minutes later carrying his backpack, sleeping bag, and a towel. Leslie tossed her gear in the rear of Jed's VW van along with the rest of her housemates' belongings, then squeezed into the backseat next to Tracy and Fury. From the amount of junk they had all brought along, it looked to Leslie like they were taking off on a two-week vacation to Mexico rather than on an overnight road trip to a beach forty miles away.

"We're right on schedule. It's just four o'clock," she said, glancing at her Swatch as Russ climbed into the front seat next to Jed. "The competition starts at seven, but we're supposed to check in between five and six."

Jed started the engine and pulled away from the curb. An hour later he pulled into a parking space at Torrance Beach.

"There's our banner. I can see it from here," Leslie shouted as she climbed out of the van and stretched her legs. She pointed to a twenty-five-foot banner with the words "Marina Bay" painted in red on it. The banner was mounted on two poles stuck in the sand on the other side of the beach. In the distance, Leslie could also see many more banners bearing the names of beaches up and down the California coast, and hordes of well-built lifeguards gathering around them.

"Now all we have to do is get all of our gear over there," Tracy complained.

"We might have to make a couple of trips," Jed pointed out.

Leslie grabbed the big beach bag filled with her personal belongings, her sleeping bag, towel, and an extra beach blanket she had thrown into the back of the van, and started out. Tracy and Fury followed, carrying their backpacks and sleeping bags. Jed and Russ took up the rear, hauling their gear and an ice chest between them.

When they reached the Marina Bay banner, the late-afternoon sun was cooling off. The trek down the beach hadn't been half as arduous as Tracy had made it out to be, Leslie thought as she threw down her stuff in one big pile.

"Anything else in the van?" she asked.

"The tent," Jed said.

"The tent?" everyone asked at once.

"What's wrong with bringing a tent? I thought we might need a tent to change in."

"Nothing. As long as I don't have to go back and get it," Fury commented.

"I'll be glad to get it," Leslie volunteered, feeling full of energy.

She was about to head back to the car when Jeff walked over and said, "Great. You're all here. Fury and Leslie need to register."

His voice sounded very detached, as if he were bored. *Well, I'll show him,* Leslie thought. That line was quickly becoming her motto, it went through her mind so often. Without a word to Jeff, she followed Fury over to the registration desk and signed in.

By the time they returned to the group,

Jed's pup tent was up—in fact, he was in it—
and Tracy and Russ were resting on their
sleeping bags while Fury was roaming about
restlessly. Other Marina Bay lifeguards, most
of whom Leslie knew at least on sight, had
also set up camp for the night under and
around the Marina Bay banner. As Leslie
spread out her blanket and put her sleeping
bag on it, she couldn't help wondering where
Jeff was planning to hang out for the night.

"Dinner time," she heard Fury announce.
Now she knew why he'd been so restless—
typical Fury.

No one needed a second call. Jed bolted out
of his tent and joined everyone around the ice
chest. They had all chipped in earlier in the
day to pack it full of sandwiches, snacks, and
drinks. Leslie looked at her Swatch. It was
already six o'clock.

Russ opened up the ice chest and started
passing out the sandwiches. Leslie took two
bites of her ham and cheese sandwich and
realized that she'd rather not eat on a nervous
stomach. She didn't want to get a cramp
during the race. Last night's spaghetti and this
morning's eggs and cereal would have to
sustain her. She gave the rest of the sandwich
back to her brother to finish. When everyone

was done eating, Tracy announced, "I've got a surprise for everybody."

Out of her backpack Tracy took a pile of She's A Beach/Marina Bay T-shirts with a silk-screen of the pier and Marina Bay on the front. "If we wear them, it'll bring Leslie and Fury good luck," she said. "Take one and pass them around. One size fits all."

Leslie took off the red sweat suit she was wearing and slipped the oversized, lucky T-shirt over her red Speedo racing suit. "Oh, Tracy. These are great. That was so sweet of you," she told her roommate.

Just then Jeff came over. "I wish I had brought a camera," he said when he noticed the whole gang in their T-shirts. "You guys look cute."

"I've got one for you, too, Jeff. It's for good luck," Tracy said, taking another T-shirt out of her backpack.

"Thanks Tracy. This group really has team spirit. Now all I need to do is round up our team. Fury and Leslie need to get down to the water."

He seems to be in a much better mood, but he's still too chicken to talk to me directly, Leslie thought as the T-shirted contingent of the Marina Bay team headed toward the water. Once they reached the shore, however, she didn't give Jeff a second thought. The scene near the ocean was so frenzied that it easily distracted her. Senior lifeguards were frantically readying boats, boards, and members of their squad. Spectators were spread out along the shoreline as far as the eye could see. Leslie noticed that several giant searchlights had been set up to light up the action in the water when it got dark. At the moment there was still enough natural light for her to spot the rest of the Marina Bay team. Like herself, they were all wearing their red Speedos. She and Fury joined Jeff and the other lifeguards at the water's edge. Leslie looked back at the crowd. She could spot Russ, Tracy, and Jed in their special shirts.

"Okay, time for a pep talk," Jeff said, gathering his team into a huddle. As Leslie stepped into it, she was more aware than ever that she was the only woman.

"I don't have to tell you that we want to win," Jeff said, getting Leslie's attention again. "But winning isn't everything as long as everyone does his best." Jeff looked at Leslie and corrected himself. "And her best. We know she's a beach, Marina Bay." Jeff pointed to the writing on his new T-shirt. "So let's show these other lifeguards what that means. Some of us have even been training after work to get ready for this competition, and I want you to know that I think it's going to pay off."

Leslie knew, even though he wasn't looking at her, that Jeff was referring to herself and Fury. Although it was the last thing she'd expected him to say, she had to admit she appreciated the recognition.

"Who's a beach?" Jeff yelled.

"Marina Bay!" came back a loud reply.

Leslie heard a loud horn blow. "Okay, let's get ready to hit the water," Jeff shouted. Twenty Marina Bay lifeguards lined up one behind the other in the order in which they would compete. The first leg was in the lifesaving boat, and Jeff was one of the two oarsmen.

Leslie was scheduled to swim in the last leg of the relay race, right behind Fury, just as they had practiced. As she watched Jeff push off in the boat, she wondered why he had put her last. She came up with two theories. If the team was way out in front, her lap wouldn't make that much of a difference, and if they were way behind, the same was true. In other words, Leslie figured, Jeff was just making sure that his team's result in the race didn't hinge on an inferior female's performance.

Leslie looked out toward the water again.

Daylight was vanishing fast. By the time her turn came, the searchlights would be on and lighting her way. She hoped the waves wouldn't be too high.

Right now the early competitors had to contend with the strong current. All the oarsmen were having a tough time keeping their boats on course, but Jeff and his partner seemed to be faring better than most, Leslie observed. Some boats had already capsized. To the cheers and shrieks of their friends and teammates, Leslie included, the two lead-off Marina Bay lifeguards streaked in to shore in second place.

Jeff leaped out of the boat and tapped the next runner.

"Great job," Fury yelled to Jeff as the runner sprinted down the beach. As he came racing back to send the first rescue-board paddler into the water, Marina Bay had dropped into third place. But the team was back in second place after the next Marina Bay swimmer finished his first lap. Two more sets of Marina Bay oarsmen, runners, paddlers, and swimmers kept up the pace and the team's position until it was time for the final foursome to complete the grueling relay race.

Nervously, Leslie shook out her limbs to relax. She could see the tension on Fury's face as he prepared himself to enter the water. Marina Bay still held second place. In a few moments Fury would take off on his paddleboard, then it would be Leslie's turn. Leslie couldn't have been more wrong in thinking her leg of the race wouldn't count all that much. The searchlights reflected off the water like giant moons as she watched Fury's board cut through the illuminated sea. Leslie felt excited and confident; their extra practice sessions just might pay off.

"Go, Fury!" she yelled.

His arms became blurs as she watched them propel the board forward. It was hard to tell for sure, but as Fury was coming in, it looked to Leslie like he had overtaken the paddler in first place. Fury grounded his board, touched her, and with what sounded like his last breath said, "Go for it, Leslie." She could tell that Fury had given it his best shot. Leslie wanted to do the same.

She raced into the water and jackknifed under a wave. The searchlights did little to brighten the surf underneath, but Leslie quickly surfaced and began swimming in a smooth, rapid rhythm. Stroke, breathe. Stroke, breathe . . . She swam out to the hundred-meter marker with all her might, changed direction underwater, and headed

back to shore. Stroke, breathe . . . she con-
centrated on keeping a steady stroke. She had
no idea where anyone else was in the water;
she heard little and saw even less. All of a
sudden she felt herself caught in a giant wave.
At first she tried to swim through it, but soon
realized it was hopeless. She held her breath
and let the wave take over. Where the wave
would carry her she didn't know. She just
wanted to finish the race in one piece.

Leslie felt the sand beneath her and staggered to her feet. The next thing she knew, she
was high above the sand, sitting on the
shoulders of four fellow Marina Bay lifeguards.
Everyone beneath her was screaming, "We
won! We won! We're number one!"

"You did it!" Fury screamed over the din.
"You were a whole lap out in front when you
came in."

From her vantage point above the crowd,
she saw Russ give her a V for victory sign, Jed,
a thumbs-up sign, and Tracy pointing with
both hands to her lucky T-shirt. Leslie smiled
and made a two-handed thumbs-up sign back.
She'd won! Marina Bay had won!

"Leslie, you were great out there," a familiar voice told her. She was back on the ground
again, face to face with Jeff. The rest of the
crowd seemed to recede into the background.

"I knew you were a great swimmer, but I had no idea you were in a league all your own," Jeff continued. "How could I have ever thought you couldn't handle a routine rescue?" He gazed into Leslie's eyes and she felt that familiar tingly feeling inside. "I guess I learned my lesson, huh? You can handle just about anything; you don't need my help."

Leslie grinned. "I'm glad you've come to your senses," she said shakily.

"It took a while, Les, but you know, I'll never again underestimate the power of a woman." Tenderly he pushed a wet strand of hair out of her eyes. "I'll never make the same mistake again."

His kiss was as warm and soft as she remembered.

"You're one heck of a woman, Leslie Stevens," he whispered.

Here's a sneak preview of *On the Edge*, book number three in the continuing ENDLESS SUMMER series from Ivy Books.

Fury pulled back a curtain and peeked outside. The sun had just come up. He considered getting up and leaving the camper, but he didn't want to disturb Rain. And, leveling with himself as he wriggled back down into his sleeping bag, he knew he had nowhere else to go.

The sound of sizzling bacon and the smell of

fresh coffee awakened him later that morning. He popped up in bed and saw Rain standing at the tiny built-in stove beside the pull-out bed. He watched her take the bacon out of the frying pan, put it on a paper plate, and crack four eggs into the bacon grease in the pan. She seemed to Fury to be as at home cooking breakfast in a Volkswagen van as some people were in a full-sized kitchen.

"How do you like your eggs?" she asked when she noticed that Fury was awake.

"Sunny side up," he said, and smiled at her. It wasn't every day that someone served him breakfast in bed. "Anything I can do to help?"

"Why don't you turn the bed back into a seat so we can eat breakfast?" Rain suggested.

Fury reached for his shirt and board shorts on the floor of the camper and slipped them on inside his sleeping bag. Then he reached into his back pocket for a comb and made an attempt to fix his unruly hair. When he thought it looked as good as Rain's, he scooted out of the bag and slipped on his high-tops.

He pushed the sleeping bags into the rear of the camper and the bed back into a seat, while Rain transformed the kitchen into a dining room by swinging a tabletop into place. Next, she set their bacon and eggs on it, along with two cups of freshly brewed coffee. As she and Fury sat down inside the cozy camper, Fury couldn't help but marvel at the vehicle's versatility.

"What do you feel like doing today?" Rain asked.

Fury took a sip of his coffee. "Well, do you think you could drive me over to where I used to live? It's only about five minutes from here. I left my bass guitar and amplifier there." As long as he was going to stick around, Fury figured he might as well move all his stuff in and make himself really comfortable. It would be fun, he thought, to sit around a campfire and play some tunes for Rain tonight. And while he was at the house, he'd have a chance to tell Jed where he was staying.

"Wow, you play the bass? That's cool. I play a little, too. Sure, we can drive over and pick it up after breakfast," Rain concurred.

When they were done, Fury offered to help clean up, but Rain insisted that there wasn't enough room in the camper for more than one cook. While she did the dishes, Fury decided to go for a walk on the beach to stretch his legs.

He headed down to the wide, sandy cove, feeling completely in tune with nature. The sun was bright—a little too bright until he slipped on his shades. But the wind was blowing slightly, and it felt good on his face. Living on the beach with Rain might be okay, Fury thought to himself. He stopped to watch the surf break around an offshore oil rig and some brown pelicans skim the ocean in search of breakfast, then continued walking until he reached the pier.

Even before he stepped onto it, he spotted several boats with surfboards jutting out of them. That, Fury thought, meant only one thing. The surf was up at the "Ranch." He had to call Nick, right away. Surfing at Rincon yesterday had been a bust, but it was always less crowded at the Hollister Ranch. Only the more experienced surfers were willing to put up with a rough boat ride just to get there. Maybe Rain could come along. She seemed adept at so many things—for all Fury knew, she could be a surfer herself.

He hurried back to the camper, hoping that Rain had finished the chores. He'd even insist on helping her, he decided, if she hadn't. But not only had she finished, the camper had been converted back to a car, and Rain was behind the wheel, ready to roll. Fury climbed in and they took off.

Heading down the highway, Fury's heart began to pound. As they turned into the

Seahorse Shores Complex, Fury realized why it had been so important for him to pick up his bass today. He wanted Tracy to see him with Rain. He wanted to make her jealous. And, to be honest about it, he knew deep down he still wanted Tracy.

"Pull up behind that BMW convertible," Fury instructed Rain as they neared Russ's house.

"Need any help?" she offered as Fury got out of the car.

"I'll be okay," he answered. He raked his hair back, trying to look cool, but his heart was still racing. All he needed now was for Tracy to answer the door. He took a deep breath and rang the bell. She opened it.

"I came to pick up my amplifier and bass," he explained quickly, trying to step inside the house.

"Who's the chick in the car?" Tracy asked, barring Fury's way.

"Oh, just a friend."

"A friend, or a girl friend? You certainly don't waste any time, Angelo De Furie."

"What's it to you?" Fury shot back.

"Actually, it's nothing to me. Nothing at all. Come on in." Tracy stepped aside to let Fury past.

In spite of what Tracy had said, Fury knew

he had made her jealous. Unfortunately, it hadn't been worth it; he felt worse than she did. Just seeing Tracy again turned his stomach inside out. He bolted upstairs to the safety of Jed's room, hoping Russ wouldn't be around.

"Knock knock. Hey, Jed. I came by to pick up my bass and amp," Fury said, stepping inside the room.

"Great. Where are you staying?" Jed asked, putting down the psychology book he was reading.

"Oh, with a friend."

"With Nick or Danny?"

"Nah, another friend. You don't know her."

"Really?" Jed said, his eyes widening. "Who? Where?"

Fury hesitated. Although he had done nothing to be ashamed of, suddenly he felt too embarrassed to answer. This wasn't at all how he, Mr. Cool, thought he'd handle the situation. It had seemed an easy enough thing to do when he had suggested to Rain that he come back and pick up his bass and amp. But now he realized that he had returned to the house too soon. He felt like an outcast.

"C'mon, Fury, you can tell me," Jed coaxed.

"In her camper at the campground just down the road," Fury mumbled.

"Oh," Jed said. "I'm glad you told me. Someone ought to know where you are."

"Well, now you know. I've got to get going. She's waiting for me in her camper."

"Can I give you a hand?" Jed offered.

"That would be cool. Thanks. Oh, wait a sec. I wanted to make a call. Can I use your phone?"

"Be my guest. I'll carry your amp out for you."

While Jed headed downstairs, Fury picked up the phone on Jed's desk and dialed Nick's number. Fury heard the phone ring, then Nick say hello on the other end.

"Hey, Nick. This is Fury. The waves must be outrageous at the Ranch. The boats are lined up at the campground almost the length of the pier. I met this girl last night and I thought it would be fun to take her over there today. Want to catch a boat ride over with us?" Fury asked, almost all in one breath. He couldn't wait to get out of the house.

"Where should we meet?" Nick asked, sounding just as excited.

As Fury made plans to meet Nick at the campground pier, Jed returned. "Hey, Fury," he whispered. "You'd better get your butt out of here. Your friend is getting hot under the collar."

"Nick, I've got to split. I'll see you in about thirty minutes," Fury said. Then he hung up the phone and turned to say good-bye to Jed.

"I'm glad you came by," Jed said.

"Yeah. Me, too. See you around." Fury picked up his bass and headed toward the front door. Just as he opened it and was about to leave, Tracy stepped out of the downstairs bathroom and came up to him.

"So, I guess you found a place to stay last night," she commented in an unfriendly tone.

"I thought what I did meant nothing to you," Fury answered. If Tracy still cared for him and was really interested in how he was doing, now was her chance to say so, Fury thought.

Tracy stared at him without speaking.

"I'd love to chat, but I've got to go. Nice talking to you," Fury said sarcastically and walked down to the camper. Tracy slammed the door behind him. Fury opened the rear door and slid his bass in next to his amp. Then he came around the side of the camper and climbed in.

"What took you so long?" Rain asked in an agitated voice.

Fury didn't like the whiny tone in her voice, but he decided to let it slide. "I was talking to my friend, Jed. Then I had to make a phone call," he explained.

"For someone who's living out of a backpack, you sure have a lot of friends," Rain remarked.

"Well, you know the old saying: 'You can't be too rich or have too many friends.' That's why I'm glad I met you," Fury said, still trying to keep his cool.

He seemed to have said the right thing. Rain smiled. "Okay, where to now?" she asked.

"I've got a great day planned for us. Nick, you, and I are going to take a boat over to Hollister Ranch to do some surfing."

"Nick? Who's Nick?"

"My surfing buddy. He's meeting us at the campground pier in thirty minutes."

"Fury, I'm not interested in spending the day with you and your *buddy*. But thanks for including me in your plans," Rain snapped.

She started the engine and pulled away from the curb. When they reached the highway, she put the gas pedal to the floor and took off.

It was obvious to Fury that he had said the wrong thing this time. "Hey, Rain, slow down. I thought you'd have a good time. Even if you don't surf, the boat ride over is a kick," he explained, trying to cheer her up. But from the way she accelerated, Fury knew he hadn't succeeded. Rain didn't say another word to him until she pulled into their campsite.

"Look, Fury, let's get something straight. I thought I'd be spending the day *alone* with you. Get it? So count me out. You can go play with your friend without me," she said, obviously still annoyed.

Fury couldn't figure where she got off being so angry at him. It wasn't as if he was trying to dump her—he had included her in his plans from the start. If anyone should be angry, he should be. He'd met her only yesterday and already she was acting as if she owned him. Maybe, he decided, it was just as well that they spent the day apart.

"What are you going to do all day?" he asked, curious.

"I'll find something. Do you mind if I play your guitar?"

"No, go ahead." Fury was glad he had his bass to bargain with.

"What time do you think you'll be back?" Rain asked as Fury took his surfboard off of the roof rack.

"Oh, the boats start heading back from Hollister around five o'clock, six the latest."

"Well, don't rush back on my account. As long as I can mess around with your bass, I'll be fine here," Rain said in a somewhat more reasonable tone of voice.

"We can sit around a campfire and I'll play you some tunes when I get back," Fury suggested.

"Sounds nice," Rain murmured.

Fury could tell that her thoughts were already on something else, but he wasn't bothered by her less-than-enthusiastic response. He hoisted his board under his arm and turned toward the ocean to check the swells. The day could only get better.

"Great. You're here," Nick said, as Fury came running down the pier toward him. "There's a boat just about to leave."

Fury and Nick raced up the dock and hopped onto the thirty-footer called the *Sea Spray*. They set down their surfboards and sat across from a row of cool-looking surfers. The boat had two long benches covered with blue flotation cushions along the gunwales, with room to stow surfboards and other equipment in the center. A small diesel engine powered the boat.

"Where's your friend?" Nick shouted to Fury over the din of the engine as the boat headed out to sea.

"She decided not to come," Fury yelled back.

With the sea spray in their faces, and the

engine churning away loudly, Fury couldn't
even talk to Nick. But it was just as well. As
the boat rocked over the waves to get beyond
where they broke, it was all he could do to
keep from getting seasick. Now he remembered why only the hale and hearty surfed
Hollister.

Once they were beyond the swells, the sea
was not at all rough; the boat steadied out,
and Fury began to enjoy the ride. He took off
his shirt to catch the hot, high-noon rays. Out
on the ocean with only blue sky and water as
far as the eye could see, he felt cut off from
civilization and, best yet, from all his petty,
everyday problems—Tracy and Rain high on
the list among them.

Before he knew it, they had reached the
Ranch and the mate was coming around to
collect the fare. He reminded the surfers to
meet the boat around five o'clock at the same
spot it had dropped them off. Fury took out his
wallet and handed the mate five dollars. Then
he took off his high-tops and shades and
stuffed them and his wallet inside his
sneakers.

The procedure was to leave your possessions on board, then drop into the water with
just your surfboard. That, Fury knew, was the
easy part. The tricky part would be meeting
the boat later, especially if the ocean got

rough. Since the boat couldn't come any closer into shore without running aground, it was that rendezvous that separated the old salts from the novices, and, in fact, added to the afternoon's excitement. But for now, Fury looked forward to dropping into the water and going in on the first big wave.

As Fury stood up on his board with Nick just a wave behind him, he thought that the only thing more beautiful than the sun-drenched day itself was the isolated stretch of sandy beach ahead of him. No blankets, beach umbrellas, litter cans, or litter, for that matter, dotted the unspoiled shore. The only people in sight were a dozen or so surfers in brightly colored board shorts, preparing to paddle back out. In no time flat, Fury and Nick were among them.

They shredded perfect waves all day, far from the crowds and the smog. It was one of those special surfing days that Fury would never forget, the kind that made him feel like he was really alive. The only thing that was wrong with the day was that it was over too soon.

When Fury saw the other surfers paddling over toward the spot where the boat would meet them, he knew it was time to go. He signaled to Nick to paddle out, and with their bellies on their boards they followed the pack out beyond the waves. They met up with the other surfers and floated on their boards as they waited for the *Sea Spray.*

For the first ten minutes Fury was as calm as the ocean; he stretched out on his long-board, belly up, to catch the last of the late-afternoon rays. But when the sun began to bother his eyes, he sat up and anxiously looked around for the boat. Some of the other surfers, he noticed, were acting restless, too, jumping off and on their boards, scanning the horizon, talking nervously to each other.

Nick paddled over to Fury. "What will we do if the boat doesn't show up?" he asked.

"Relax, dude," Fury told Nick. "It'll show up. And if it doesn't, the worst that can happen is that we have to sleep on the beach overnight."

"That could be fun."

"Eventually someone will come to get us. They have to. We paid for a round-trip ticket."

Nick grinned appreciatively. Fury's attempt to make light of the situation appeared to have made Nick feel less anxious. Fury smiled back at him, but inside he wasn't feeling nearly as self-assured as he looked or sounded.

When Rain had asked him what time he'd be back, he had told her between five and six o'clock. If he didn't show up, for all he knew she'd get ticked off at him again and do something impulsive like take off without him. After how strangely she'd acted this morning, he really couldn't predict what she'd do. But then, it occurred to him, how could he? He'd only met her yesterday.

Fury groaned. How could he have been so stupid? If he didn't know her all that well, why had he left his bass and amp and the rest of his worldly possessions with her? Maybe she never had any intention of waiting for him today. She could take off with everything he owned whenever she felt like it. It all made sense now: why she had cooperated with him about picking up the bass, why she had made such a stink about Nick, why she had asked him what time he was coming back. What a fool he'd been! She had even admitted to him that she played the bass!

To add to his problems, the wind picked up, and Fury started to shiver from the cold. Relax, he told himself. You're letting your fears run away with you. The boat will be along any minute. You'll be back at the campground before you know it. Everything will be all right; everything, including Rain's camper, will be there.

"Maybe we should head back to shore. I'm getting cold," Nick suggested, apparently feeling the drop in temperature himself.

Fury looked around to see what the other surfers were doing. Some of them had formed a circle with their boards and seemed to be discussing what to do next.

"Let's find out what the other surfers are doing," Fury suggested.

Nick nodded in agreement. They paddled over and joined the huddle.

"It's five-twenty now. I think we should wait until five-thirty," one older-looking surfer said, glancing at his waterproof Casio. "If the boat doesn't come by then, we might as well get out of the water and get warm."

Everyone, including Fury and Nick, seemed to think this was a sensible suggestion. But when the boat hadn't arrived by five-twenty-five, Fury was shaking uncontrollably.

"I've got to go in. I'm really cold," he informed Nick.

"I'll go with you," his buddy said.

Fury and Nick broke away from the pack and started paddling in toward shore.

"Hey, you guys, the boat's coming!" the older-looking surfer shouted to them when they were almost halfway there.

They paddled back frantically. Fury's arms felt like rubber, but he made it to the boat in time, and one of the surfers helped lift him out of the water and over the side of the boat.

Once all the surfers were safe on board, the mate handed out blankets. He explained, "The captain would like to apologize for the delay. Some seaweed got caught in our cool-water intake and we had to cut our speed. We'll have to take it easy on our way back as well."

As long as he had a blanket around him, Fury didn't care how fast they went. The only thing that mattered to him now was that he was out of the water and warm. But as soon as the boat docked at the campground pier he had another, much more pressing priority.

"I need you to do me a big favor, Nick," Fury said as he threw off the blanket and threw on his T-shirt and high-tops. "Come with me over to the campsite where I'm staying."

"Sure. Why?"

"Just come with me. I'll explain later," Fury said.

Fury snatched up his surfboard and flew down the gangplank and across the hard-packed sand toward Rain's campsite at the far end of the beach. Nick followed right behind. Even before Fury reached the section of the campground where the RVs were allowed to park, he slowed to a fast walk and breathed a sigh of relief. He could see Rain's distinctive yellow-and-white VW pulled up in her campsite in the distance.

"So, what gives?" Nick asked, catching up to Fury.

"It's no big deal. I just had a funny feeling when we were in the water waiting for the boat to pick us up that Rain had taken off with all my stuff. I guess it was just part of my general panic," Fury explained as they reached the camper.

"Well, you can breathe easy now," Nick commented when he saw all of Fury's gear, the amp and bass included, lined up outside the camper.

Fury looked down and saw his stuff spread out on the ground. Why was it here and not inside? he wondered.

The side door of the camper slid open and a guy Fury had seen the day before at the beach bums' camp stepped out.

"Rain told me to tell you you've been replaced. So collect your stuff and start moving," he said in a rough voice.

"Tell him thanks for letting me play his bass," Rain called out from inside the camper.

"She told me to tell you thanks for—"

"I heard her," Fury said, interrupting.

"And tell him that I'm sorry I won't be able to hear him play tonight. But he really bummed me out," she explained.

"Tell her to tell me herself," Fury shouted

back, as angry with himself as he was with Rain. All he could think about now was how dumb he'd been to trust a perfect stranger and not to trust his girl friend, Tracy.

"C'mon, Fury, cool it," Nick said as he put down his surfboard, picked up Fury's pack, and hoisted it on his back. "Let's get out of here."

"You'd better listen to your friend," the beach bum threatened.

"I'll carry the amp," Nick offered. "You take your bass."

Nick started walking back toward the pier where he had parked his car. "Good thing I came along. Now I know why you wanted me to," Nick commented when Fury caught up with him.

"Yeah. Good thing," Fury said, still frustrated with Rain's sudden change of heart.

Now where was he going to sleep tonight? He didn't have anywhere to go, and his luck had run out. Could he ever make it up to everyone in the house so he could move back in?